THE THREAD OF ARIADNE:

The Labyrinth of the Calendar of Minos

THE THREAD OF ARIADNE:
The Labyrinth of the Calendar of Minos

CHARLES F. HERBERGER

PHILOSOPHICAL LIBRARY
New York

Copyright, © 1972, by Philosophical Library, Inc.,
15 East 40th Street, New York, N. Y. 10016

All rights reserved

Library of Congress Catalog Card No. 72-78167

SBN 8022-2089-4

Manufactured in the United States of America

To MELVINA

"Crete is fair and fertile, sea-girt. Therein are many men, countless men, and ninety cities. They have a mixture of languages. For there are Achaeans, stout-hearted Eteocretans, Kydonians, Dorians with their three tribes, godlike Pelasgians. There too is Knossos, a mighty city, where Minos used to be king for nine years, a familiar of mighty Zeus."

—Homer, *The Odyssey*

TABLE OF CONTENTS

Chapter		Page
I.	The Mythopoeic Way of Thought	15
II.	Principal Patterns in Minoan Religion	20
III.	A Border Inspection	39
IV.	Threading the Labyrinth	52
V.	The Seasons of the Sun and the Festivals of the Moon	63
VI.	Bull, Lion, Serpent, and Griffon	77
VII.	Theseus and Ariadne	88
VIII.	Beyond the Pillars of Hercules	104
IX.	The Tragic Games of Love and Death	118
X.	Daidalos	131
XI.	Eclipses and the Hyperboreans	139
Appendix		152
Bibliography		156

LIST OF ILLUSTRATIONS

Plate I. Restoration of Toreador Fresco.
First Version made for Sir Arthur Evans.
Plate II. Restoration of Toreador Fresco.
Second Version made for Sir Arthur Evans.
Plate III. Restoration of Toreador Fresco in Heraclion Museum.
Plate IV. Diagram of restored border of Toreador Fresco.
Fig. 1. Pattern illustrating synthesis.
Fig. 2. Figurine from Knossos.
Fig. 3. Engraved seal from Crete.
Fig. 4. Motif on sealing from Phaistos.
Fig. 5. Figurine from Knossos.
Fig. 6. Figurine from Knossos.
Fig. 7. Figurine from Crete.
Fig. 8. Engraved gem from Crete.
Fig. 9. Engraved prism bead from Crete.
Fig. 10. Engraved prism bead from Crete.
Fig. 11. Engraved cylinder seal from Knossos.
Fig. 12. Clay sealing from Knossos.
Fig. 13. Clay sealing from Knossos.
Fig. 14. Motif on sealing from Zakros.
Fig. 15. Engraved seal from Knossos district.
Fig. 16. (a), (b). Motifs on seal from Knossos.
Fig. 17. Motif on seal from Crete.
Fig. 18. Related motifs from Cretan seals.
Fig. 19. (a). Engraved cylinder seal from Crete.
Fig. 19. (b). Motif on seal illustrated in Fig. 19 (a).
Fig. 20. Fresco in Palace at Phaistos.
Fig. 21. (a), (b). Ivory seal from Platanos.
Fig. 22. (a), (b). Ivory seal from Kalathiana.

Fig. 23. Schematic diagram of calendar.
Fig. 24. Table of seasons and festivals.
Fig. 25. Relief fresco from Knossos.
Fig. 26. Motif on seal from Crete.
Fig. 27. Motifs on seal from Knossos.
Fig. 28. Motif on seal from Zakros.
Fig. 29. Fresco fragment from Knossos.
Fig. 30. Engraved talismanic gem from Crete.
Fig. 31. Engraved talismanic gem from Siteia.
Fig. 32. Gold signet ring from Knossos.
Fig. 33. Bronze cult object from Tylissos.
Fig. 34. Gold signet ring from Arkhanes.
Fig. 35. The Chieftan's Cup from Agia Triada.
Fig. 36. Engraved gem from Psychro Cave.
Fig. 37. Plan of East Wing of Palace at Knossos.
Fig. 38. Fresco fragment from Knossos.
Fig. 39. Fresco fragment from Knossos.
Fig. 40. Fresco fragment from Knossos.
Fig. 41. Diagram of Table of Offerings from Phaistos.
Fig. 42. Table of Measurements.
Fig. 43. The Court of the Stone Spout where the Toreador Fresco was found.

ACKNOWLEDGMENTS

Appreciation is expressed by the author to the copyright holders for permission to reproduce twelve drawings from *Cretan Seals* by V. E. G. Kenna (Clarendon Press, Oxford, 1960); for two illustrations from *Sir Arthur Evans' Knossos Fresco Atlas* by Mark Cameron and Sinclair Hood (Gregg International Publishers Limited, 1967); and to W. W. Norton & Company Inc., New York, for permission to reproduce one illustration from their edition of *The Archaeology of Crete* by J. D. S. Pendlebury (1965).

The author also wishes to express his gratitude to Mr. R. W. Hamilton, Keeper of the Ashmolean Museum, Oxford, for his kindness in making available materials in the museum archives. He is also most grateful to his friends, David and Priscilla Henken, whose timely gift of a book materially influenced this research.

THE THREAD OF ARIADNE:

The Labyrinth of the Calendar of Minos

Chapter I

THE MYTHOPOEIC WAY OF THOUGHT

The seed from which this book grew was the discovery that the well known Toreador Fresco, unearthed by Sir Arthur Evans at the Palace of Minos in Crete, combined symbols and numerical relationships that corresponded mathematically and mythically so exactly with solar and lunar cycles and with the context of Minoan myth and iconography that I was compelled to conclude that it was, in fact, a ritual calendar. Presenting that discovery is the chief aim of this book. But since Minoan culture was theocratic and the ritual calendar central in the design of its religious fabric, it was inevitable that in pursuing the thread of the calendar many other dark corners of the labyrinth of Minoan culture were illuminated from a fresh perspective in the search. I should also like to add that from the beginning my interest in this subject was motivated by something more than a merely antiquarian curiosity about a prehistoric culture. Minoan art and architecture charmed me, and as a unified vision of the Minoan world picture gradually took shape before me, I was struck by the contrast it presented not only to our present industrial vision but to the classical culture of Greece which it antedated by a thousand years. It awakened me to a sense of values and a human orientation toward the cosmos radically different in basic assumptions from the Classical-Judeo-Christian tradition that has dominated the Western World since the time of Homer and the book of Genesis. It was not merely that the Minoans accepted a different standard of ethical values. Their very processes of thought and feeling were different from ours. That is to say their psychic life was different—and different in a way that I found refreshing, healthy, and human by contrast with the apparent spiritual malaise of our contemporary world.

It is necessary to make at once clear distinctions between the way in which the Minoans ordinarily thought and felt and the way in which we are accustomed to think and feel by our training and environment. This is true for two reasons. First because it is impossible to get a true picture of their vision of life without making the effort—and it does take some effort—to see, as it were, through their eyes and exercise their patterns of thought and feeling. Secondly because I have frequently found it necessary to adopt their way of relating and connecting things to make my presentation intelligible.

We are trained from childhood to separate fact from fancy and thinking from feeling—in the commendable pursuit of truth, of course—so that we attempt to live—although not always very successfully—a compartmentalized psychic life in which, by fits and starts, we adjust to facts and suppress fancy or indulge fancy and forget facts, or exercise our reason while excluding feeling or unleash our feelings while taking a respite from reason. On the other hand, the Minoan tendency—quite apparent in their art and religion—was to combine empirical facts with imaginative fancies and to think in rhythm with their feeling and feel in rhythm with their thinking. I have, of course, deliberately stated the extremes to make the contrast sharp, but I believe the generalization is essentially valid.

I should like to make one further distinction on a more technical plane. It appears to me that there are two kinds of thinking which as human beings we are all more or less capable of. One is what is commonly called analysis. Analysis is a method of understanding things by noting their differences and separating them. The strategy is to divide and conquer. We say that John is not Mary and Mary is not John. We could take a further step and say that John is John, a particular unity identifiable as such. And although in ordinary situations we would not be likely to do so, we could say that John is not both John and not John. In making these simple statements, although we might not be aware of it, we have established the three underlying principles of Aristotelian logic upon which the whole structure of what we ordinarily consider rational thought is based. Stated more abstractly we have three propositions. A is A. In formal logic this is known as the principle of identity. A is not B. This is known as the principle of contradiction. And finally we have: A is not both A and not A. This is called the principle of the excluded middle. This kind of analytic thinking we use every day—in an informal fashion, of course, and in highly complex combinations, permutations, and sequences.

There is also another kind of thinking which we all use to some extent. It is also orderly and deserving of our respect. But it is based upon a different set of assumptions and it utilizes different principles from Aristotelian logic. It is what I should call the method of synthesis. Analysis proceeds by taking things out of their total context, assigning terms to them, and noting their differences. Synthesis is a method of putting things together rather than taking them apart. Furthermore, synthesis always orders things within a total context so that terms have meaning only in relation to other terms in the same context rather than in isolation as absolute unities. Through analysis we come to know parts. Through synthesis we come to know wholes.

By analogy with the three first principles of formal logic we can construct three parallel but different principles of synthesis. Complementary to the analytical principle of identity is the synthetic principle of analogy. Whatever is the same is the same not by identity but by analogy. For instance, we can say John is not absolutely the same as Peter, but both being men, they are relatively the same. That is, as men, they share an analogous form.

Complementing the analytical principle of contradiction is the synthetic principle of polarity. Whatever is different is different not by contradiction but by opposition. For instance, the word "up" has meaning only in a context in which its polar opposite "down" is also recognized. The word "up" does not contradict the word "down" but each is needed to complete the meaning of the other.

Finally, the analytical principle of the excluded middle is complemented by the synthetic principle of the included middle. Relations are not excluded from each other, but included in each other. The total meaning of any part of a context depends upon its relation to every other part of that context and hence to the whole. And this is true for each part. Each part includes in its meaning every other part. Any part is therefore not absolutely itself but relatively itself.

The principles of synthesis are well illustrated by the diagram in Figure 1. If we disregard our knowledge that A and B are letters of the alphabet and look at the diagram simply as an abstract pattern, we may apply the principles of synthesis to discover its meaning as a pattern. The meaning of any particular A or particular B includes its relation to all the other A's and B's. The various A's and B's are the same not by identity but by analogy—analogous shape and position. A is not every other A, but it is like every other A. The A's and B's are not different by contradiction but by complementation. No pattern, and hence no meaning, would exist if the A's did not provide it for the B's and the B's for the A's. Finally, the meaning of any particular letter in the context includes the meaning of all the others. Neither the A's nor the B's have any meaning apart from the integrated pattern of which each is an essential part. Remove any part and you have affected the synthetic meaning of the whole.

I have taxed the reader with this somewhat lengthy exposition because I believe it will help to clarify an important difference between the way in which we are accustomed to face our most crucial problems in life and the way that, on the evidence of their art and thought, the Minoans must have customarily approached theirs. Consciously or unconsciously we all make use of both analysis and synthesis in our thinking and there is no reason to believe that the Minoans used one method to the exclusion of the other. But there is a rather marked difference in the emphasis placed upon one or the other by the two cultures and in the degree of trust invested in them. Such a difference in emphasis and trust can have far reaching consequences for a society. The poet, the artist, the musician, the mystic, and the myth maker, by virtue of the medium in which he works and the ends he works for, tends to exercise his synthetic faculties to a high degree. The logician, the scientist, the engineer, the technician, and the mechanic, by virtue of his medium and ends, tends to develop his analytic faculties highly and leave his synthetic faculties untouched. The emphasis of Minoan culture was on the former; the emphasis of industrial society is on the latter. Accordingly, if we wish to gain something more than a distorted view of the Minoan way of thinking, we will have to make an allowance for this difference in emphasis and not merely conclude that the Minoans were trying to think as we do, but making a dreadful botch of it.

In the matters which they considered most important in life, they generally thought synthetically. They looked for correspondences between all things—a tiny spiral murex shell and the spiralling milky way. They were impressed by the opposition and polarity of sun and moon, of male and female, of life and death. And they sought to find meaning in the entire cosmic context of life considered as one great drama and design with infinite complexity in detail but one recurring plot varied by a limited number of motifs. This particular use of synthetic thinking has been aptly called mythopoeic thought.

Mythopoeic thinking is the normal way of thinking among primitive peoples. It is also, allowing for increased sophistication, the way that poets think, and have always thought, when they are thinking within the context of a given poem. It is not an outmoded way of thought, and it is by no means inferior to analytic thinking. But it is different from analytic thinking. It will be frequently necessary to think mythopoeically if one desires to follow the thread of meaning in the chapters to come.

Chapter II

PRINCIPAL PATTERNS IN MINOAN RELIGION

The ritual calendar to be examined later abounds in symbolic references to mythic motifs in Minoan religion. Its interpretation depends in part upon mathematical correspondences with the facts of astronomy and in part upon approaching it within the mythic context of which it is a part. To provide such a context is the aim of this chapter.

Minoan religion, as might be expected, underwent a gradual evolution from its beginnings in the Neolithic Period or earlier, to a stage of high development in the Bronze Age, and finally into a decline as it was gradually superseded by Olympian Greek religion to which it contributed some important features. The fresco calendar in question dates from the Late Bronze Age. Its more precise dating will be discussed later. For present purposes it is only necessary to note that it was a byproduct of Minoan religious culture in the stage immediately preceding its decline and consequently embodies much that was essential to that religion in its period of highest development. The schematic picture of Minoan religion which follows is drawn to show its synthetic fabric and its central elements and makes no attempt to be exhaustive in detail nor to trace its evolution.

The most prominent feature of Minoan religion is the dominance of a feminine deity—the goddess whom Sir Arthur Evans called the "Great Goddess." She is the great cosmic mother of all being and hence her attributes are all-inclusive and being all-inclusive, even contradictory. R. F. Willetts describes her aptly as follows: "The goddess is represented in a rich variety of associations: with animals, birds and snakes; with the baetylic pillar and the sacred tree; with the poppy and the lily; with the sword and the double-axe. She is a huntress and a goddess of sports; she is armed and she presides over ritual dances; she has dominion over mountain, earth, sky and sea; over life and death; she is household-goddess, vegetation-goddess, Mother and Maid. She is, like the figurines shaped by human hands out of which she grew, an eclectic figure. But her dominance in all spheres also demonstrates that she operated, in all her particular associations, as an abstract and unifying principle. She is both one and many."[1]

As a unifying principle she stands for continuity by incorporating polar oppositions in her nature. She is the source of all creation and likewise of disintegration and death. Her being is the matrix of the universe itself—self-generating, self-perpetuating, and self-consuming. The rhythm of her ever-changing but ever-recurring movements is seen in the cycles of the seasons, of the astronomical bodies, and the vegetable, animal, and human cycles of birth, mating, death, and rebirth.

In her astronomical aspect she is closely associated with the moon. This is not difficult to understand. The moon is in continual motion and undergoes a regularly recurring cycle of transformations—new moon, full moon, old moon. In parallel fashion the goddess is virgin, mother, and hag. The moon is white and the goddess' color in artistic representations is usually white as, indeed, all females are conventionally rendered in Minoan frescoes. Furthermore, the monthly lunar cycle from new moon to new moon closely parallels the normal feminine menstrual cycle. For all of these reasons—and some more abstruse to be discussed later—the goddess is viewed as a moon-goddess.

Another aspect of the goddess of particular importance to the calendar is her association in art, iconography, and myth with certain mystical numbers. This fact appears not to be generally known to students of Minoan religious iconography, but it can be amply demonstrated by reference to archaeological finds. In Minoan art and in later mythology of Minoan derivation she—or the later goddesses into which she was fractured —is consistently associated with odd numbers, which appear to have been considered feminine as opposed to even numbers which were considered male. This tradition was still alive in classical times among the Pythagoreans, who built their entire philosophical system on a metaphysics of number.[2] According to the classical biographer, Porphyrius, Pythagoras went to Crete and was initiated in the mysteries of the Idaean Dactyls, guardians of the secret Orphic doctrine, whose cult center was the Idaean Cave, the reputed birth place of the Bronze Age and pre-classical Cretan Zeus. Dactyls, of course, means "fingers" and more specifically the five fingers of the hand, or each hand, making ten in all, as can be seen in the late Minoan clay figurines of the goddess, holding up both hands displaying the five fingers of each in a symbolic gesture. (Fig. 2) Robert Graves argues convincingly in his *White Goddess* that Pythagoras derived the germ of his number mysticism from this remnant of Minoan religion still surviving in classical times and my findings confirm this view.[3]

Although the goddess is associated with odd numbers in general, my research has revealed her most frequently associated with three, five, seven, eleven, and multiples thereof. We have already seen that she was associated with the five Dactyls. Additional light is provided by consulting the Greek myth of Cronos and Rhea. Cronos and Rhea were the mythical parents of Zeus, which probably reflects their antiquity as divinities surviving from a religion antecedent to the Olympian religion of Greece in which Zeus was the preeminent divinity. According to myth Rhea created the five Dactyls as attendants on her lover Cronos, "while Zeus was still an infant in the Dictaean Cave."[4]

Another Greek tradition associating Crete, the Goddess, and five Dactyls is the mythic founding of the Olympic Games. We have already seen that the Goddess presided over ritual sports and dances. The tradition is that Herakles, whose name is derived from the Cretan Goddess, Hera, was the founder of the Olympic Games, a religious calendric festival which he transplanted from Crete.[5] R. F. Willetts writes, "Herakles brought with him from Crete, to found the Olympic Games, his companions Paionios, Epimedes, Idas, and Iasios. Of these, Idas is clearly named after Cretan Mount Ida and Iasios recalls the Iasion whom we shall find featured in the earliest attested form of the sacred marriage."[6] Willetts is concerned here with the ritual sports attendant upon celebration of the symbolic marriage of the Minoan goddess to her consort of which more will be said later. But I should like to point out that Herakles, whom a later tradition connects with the phallic thumb, is accompanied by four companions, like four fingers making with the thumb five in all, and recalling the Cretan Dactyls once again. This identification is supported by Pausanius who reports that the Dactyls were worshipped at Elis under the names of Herakles, Paeonius, Epimedes, Jasius, and Idas.[7]

But let us look at a few archaeological examples. In the Ashmolean Museum at Oxford is a small, dark brown, cornelian seal stone which is dated from the Middle Minoan Age (c. 2000-1500 B.C.). It is illustrated by photograph in V. E. G. Kenna's *Cretan Seals,* which serves as a catalogue for the Ashmolean collection, and is labeled there no. 127 (A.M. 1938. 1144). The seal is in the shape of a hand with a bracelet about the wrist. The fingers are delicately carved and notably plump and unmasculine. It appears to represent the five-fingered hand of the goddess. This is further borne out by the engraved base, used for making impressions in clay sealings. The engraving shows a long-necked and long-beaked water fowl with slender legs, which is probably a crane, a bird which we will later see is closely associated with the goddess. In addition, there are two opposed circular symbols, which represent the moon goddess and her consort, the sun. This interpretation is supported by the small bucranium (bull's skull) engraved within one circle, identifying it as the solar bull (a motif to be discussed later), while the second circle is unfilled to represent the full moon, spouse of the sun and the goddess herself. (Fig. 3)

Although the Dactyl or five-fingered hand motif is frequently related to the goddess, it is not the only motif that suggests her association with the mystic number five. There is a sealing in the Archaeological Museum of Heraclion in Crete (Gallery III, Case 40, no. 781) which displays an interesting type of five-pointed star. (Fig. 4) It was found at the Palace of Phaistos and is dated as Middle Minoan (c. 2000-1700 B.C.). The remarkable feature of this pentagonal star is that its outline is interwoven in such a way that one can follow it infinitely without arriving at an end in the manner of a circle. This design recalls the eternal return aspect of the goddess and we may therefore be reasonably sure that it was intended to be emblematic of her nature.

The most impressive works of art reflecting the symbolic numbers of the goddess are the so-called "snake goddesses." As we have seen the snake was one of several animals especially sacred to the Great Goddess. It is therefore unlikely that these "snake goddesses" are evidences of a minor cult unrelated to the central feminine deity. There are two excellently preserved miniature statues in faience from Knossos in this category. They may be seen in the Heraclion Museum (Gallery IV, Case 50) and are dated Middle Minoan to Late Minoan I (c. 1700-1450 B.C.). It is worth noting that both were found in the central shrine of the Palace at Knossos and we may therefore infer that they are religious icons of importance to the official religion of the state. One of these goddesses stands with arms outstretched holding in each hand a sacred serpent. Her breasts are bared in the Minoan fashion and she wears a girdle and apron over a long skirt with seven concentric flounces. Among the Pythagoreans the number seven was sacred to the goddess Athene and signified intelligence, health, and light.[8] Athene is a goddess of pre-Olympian origin and, in fact, she is probably the Potnia Atana (our Lady of Athens) mentioned in a Linear B tablet listing offerings made at Knossos in the period of the Mycenaean occupation of the palace (c. 1400-1100 B.C.).[9] This identification is further confirmed by the classical tradition associating Athene with a sacred beneficial snake. But our concern for the moment is simply to show that the seven flounces of her skirt are intended to have symbolic significance. (Fig. 5)

The other faience statue from Knossos shows the goddess standing with arms held forward, palms upward, as if offering life and fertility. The expression on her face is benevolent, and sacred serpents twine about both of her arms and one climbs up her triple spiralled tiara to show his head from its top. Her skirt is without flounces, but another mystic number, again an odd number, is indicated by her triple tiara. (Fig. 6)

There is also the well-known gold and ivory goddess in the Boston Museum of Fine Arts. The original provenance of this statue is unknown, but so authoritative an expert as J. D. S. Pendlebury considers it a genuine Minoan work and he dates it Late Minoan I. The goddess stands with bared breasts, and arms held forward, holding two sacred serpents each of which is wound spirally three folds about her forearms. She wears a flounced skirt below her belt and each of five flounces is edged with a gold border. Here again we find two of her significant numbers, three and five. (Fig. 7)

It would be possible to cite many other examples of odd numbers, and particularly three, five, and seven—and less frequently yet significantly, eleven—used in an emblematic way to signify the goddess. But the above examples together with others to be referred to later in connection with other problems in iconography should be sufficient to show that mystic numbers are a significant factor in Minoan religion.

In the earliest stage of Minoan religion the goddess appears to have had no male divinity as a counterpart. Later when a male divinity does appear on the scene, he is clearly in a subordinate position to the goddess. As many scholars have observed, this probably reflects a society that was matrilinear, i.e., inheritance by virtue of mother right rather than from father to son. This will assume more importance when we come to discuss the Minoan king's relationship to religion. At present our concern is with the male divininty, who, however, significantly derives his godhead by virtue of being the son of the goddess. But he is also her young consort joined with her in a sacred marriage and he is associated with the male functions in reproduction and fertility.

It may seem strange that he has no father, but this is mythically understandable if we recall that he is, in an ultimate sense, only one aspect of the great goddess herself who was originally androgynous and self-perpetuating. A later echo of the bipolar sexuality of the goddess is the mythical figure of Androgeos, son of the goddess and King Minos. Androgeos was slain by the Athenians and as retribution Minos extracted from them a tribute of seven young men and seven maidens every eight years to be victims of the Minotaur in the Cretan Labyrinth. Androgeos, as his name implies, was androgynous, i.e., both male and female as the goddess, his mother, was originally.

The male divinity was thus originally an attribute of the goddess which in time came to be differentiated in the figure of a son and youthful consort. Even so his ultimate dependence upon her is mythically expressed by his mortality. He is a god who dies and is reborn with the vegetation cycle of the seasons and the solar cycle of the year. He is, in fact, one more example of the archetype of the dying god so familiar from the mythologies of the ancient Middle East.

R. F. Willetts, referring to Frazer's *Golden Bough,* describes him as follows: "The researches of Frazer demonstrated the connexion between the youthful god and agrarian magic. This god must die so that the crops may live. Crops have to be sown, brought to their seasonal maturity in the fields by the operation of nature, and then harvested. The operation begins again with the seed, gathered and preserved after the harvest, then returned to the earth at the proper time. The element of continuity in this vegetation cycle is represented by the goddess, who also maintains the continuity of human life. The element of discontinuity, of growth, decay and renewal, is a god. He is male because he personifies the seed and, because he shares in its mortality, he is a dying god. And he dies as the son or the lover of the goddess. Hence Evans, in commenting upon the mortal character of the Cretan god, wrote: 'That his death and return to life were of annual celebration in relation to the seasonal re-birth of Nature is an almost irresistible conclusion.' The Cretan goddess and the youthful Cretan god are involved in the same essential pattern of Oriental ritual which gave rise to the myths of Ishtar and Tammuz, Isis and Osiris, Venus and Adonis."[10]

The Minoan male god was also a solar divinity as is appropriate for him as consort of the moon-goddess and as the fructifying sun which in spring warms the earth's body to germination and in a yearly death at the December solstice leaves the earth in winter's sleep. In both myth and the iconography of art he is conceived as a solar bull joined in a sacred marriage with the goddess as lunar cow.

The myth of Pasiphae is helpful here. Pasiphae ("She who shines on all") was, according to Pausanias, the moon. In the myth, Pasiphae, wife of Minos, conceives an unnatural passion for a bull sent to Minos in answer to his prayers. Minos had promised to sacrifice the bull, but he was so impressed by its size and strength that he put it to stud among his herd and sacrificed another bull in its place. His punishment was his wife's secret passion for the bull. Daidalos, the clever designer of the Labyrinth, to please Pasiphae, constructed a hollow wooden cow and covered it with the hide of a cow he had skinned and then put it in the pasture where the bull grazed. Pasiphae climbed into the wooden cow and the bull coupled with it. As a result she gave birth to Asterios ("Starry One"), who had the head of a bull and the body of a man. This was the famous Minotaur ("Minos-bull") whom Minos put in the center of the Labyrinth.

This myth not only reflects the sacred marriage of the sun and the moon and the fertility cult aspect of that marriage but also in the figure of the Minotaur connects the solar bull divinity with the human kings of Knossos whose royal title was Minos, just as the royal title of the kings of Egypt was Pharaoh. It also relates the sun-king and the moon-goddess to a mysterious maze known as the Labyrinth. But of this, more later.

The Minos of Knossos appears to have been a priest-king who was vested with a semi-divine status as the temporal incarnation of the solar bull and the consort of the great goddess. A considerable body of evidence from Minoan art and other sources confirms this conclusion. Furthermore, sacred kingship is a familiar institution in ancient Middle Eastern fertility religions with which Minoan religion shows so many parallels. R. F. Willets writes, "As the bearer of a divine title, the Cretan Minos could be compared with the divine 'priest-kings' of the religious centres of Anatolia, who represented a god, wore his dress, wielded his authority and often bore his name."[11]

There are a number of particular motifs associated with the priest-king which help to explain his relationship to the grand design of Minoan myth and religion. A motif of very high frequency which appears with a multitude of variations is what I shall call the bull-lion circle. A good example of this motif from the Late Minoan Age is a seal in the Ashmolean (A.M. 1938. 1069) which Kenna's catalogue labels no. 321. The seal shows a bull-man chased by a lion-man in a torsional circular design like a swastika. (Fig. 8) The bull-man is clearly the Minotaur of mythic fame and as son of Pasiphae, the moon-goddess, he represents one aspect of the sacred solar king. The pursuit of the bull-man by the lion-man in a circle of eternal return is emblematic of an important feature of Minoan kingship. The Minoan king is a bull-man, but he is also a lion-man. And since in addition he is a sun-king, he undergoes a yearly cycle of death and rebirth. As bull he is the waxing year from the winter solstice to the summer solstice and as lion he is the waning year from summer solstice to winter solstice—the destroyer of the bull.

What we have here is a tanist relationship between two twin king's of the year of a type that has many other parallels in other primitive religions. Castor and Pollux, Romulus and Remus, Triptolemus and Demophoon, Cain and Abel and even the Celtic Sir Gawayne and the Green Knight are examples of this archetype. The sun-king, who is also the fertility-king of his people, must die so that the crops may grow. His vitality must be renewed twice yearly at the solstices by a ritual symbolic death usually celebrated by festivals and accompanied with the sacrifice of either a human victim in his stead or an animal symbolic of his divinity. It is a natural inference that a bull was probably sacrificed at the summer solstice as a surrogate for the Minos. It is apparent then that the Minoan kingship was closely tied by festival and ritual with the calendar and most particularly with its solar aspect.

As we have seen, the goddess was associated with certain mystic numbers. This is true of the sun-god as well, except that his numbers are always even numbers and most particularly two, four, and eight and their multiples. The priest-king, as incarnation of the sun-god, also shares these mystic numbers. This numerical association can be illustrated by reference to a seal in the Ashmolean dated as Middle Minoan. The seal is in the shape of a three-sided prism bead (A.M. A.E. 1223. Cat. no. 65). The first side is engraved with a bull's skull flanked by two eight-rayed sun symbols—suggesting the waxing and the waning year. (Fig. 9) The second side bears a pattern of four lozenges decorated with crosses and separated one from the other by upright members. When later evidence is at our disposal, I believe it will be seen that this abstract pattern has reference to a period of eight years. The third side shows an S-spiral with a papyrus bud springing from each end. The spiral suggests eternal return and the papyrus buds, fertility. The symbolic numbers are, of course, two, four and eight.

It would be possible to multiply examples of this association of the sun-king with the numbers two, four, and eight and their multiples by references to Cretan art from the early Middle Minoan Period to the Late Minoan Period and indeed beyond that into the dark ages following the Trojan War and even into classical times. But the above example should suffice for the time being, since further examples will be referred to later in connection with other problems.

We have already had occasion to note that Daidalos was not only responsible for the mating of Pasiphae (moon) and the bull (sun) but also that he designed the Labyrinth in the center of which the Minotaur was placed. The Labyrinth derives its name from "labrys" meaning double axe. The double-headed axe was a ritual axe with symbolic significance. This is clear from its frequent appearance in Minoan art in a context with shrines and altars or standing in the center of another ritual object, the so-called horns of consecration. What the symbolic value of the double axe was for the Minoans we ought not to be too hasty in concluding. Like all Minoan symbols it was probably emblematic and, hence, multivalued rather than allegorical and single valued. In other words, it probably had many associations of a kind which did not contradict but enriched and complemented one another. This is true of most Minoan motifs as I have attempted to suggest in my opening chapter. To approach such an emblematic design by insisting that it must mean either this or that, and if this, not that, is an error too frequently made by the modern analytic mind. It is more fruitful to approach such emblems in their total context of possible associations wherein it often happens that they mean both this and that and more. For the moment I shall content myself with pointing out a few possible associations of the double axe with the warning that these need not complete its significance.

It is likely that it was at one time a sacrificial weapon actually used in beheading human victims representing the sacred king and the dying god of the year. Its two blades are significant because, facing in opposite directions, they imply that it cuts both ways. If we recall that the sacred sun-king is bull and lion by turns and that each destroys the other in the circle of the year, it is not difficult to see in the double sacrificial axe the blade that slays the bull and also the blade that slays the slayer.

It seems probable that in more advanced stages in Minoan religious evolution the double axe was used in sacrificing a bull or perhaps merely displayed as a symbol at the festival in which sacrifices of animals took place. A double axe pictured above a bull's head between the horns is a frequent motif in Minoan art from the Early Minoan Age to the Late Minoan Age. (Fig. 10) A good Late Minoan example from Knossos (H.M. 337) is a seal stone which is fragmentary but, nevertheless, complete enough to be clear. (Fig. 11) As this seal illustrates, the double axe was associated with the bull and more precisely with the opening between his horns. At Knossos at the Shrine of the Double Axes two horn-shaped cult objects which Evans named "horns of consecration" occupied the most prominent position on the altar of the shrine and both had sockets between the horns apparently for inserting the handles of double axes. A steatite double axe was found lying beside one of these horns.

A further step in interpretation of this obviously sacred and evidently important symbol can be made by noticing the shape of the double axe, particularly in the simplified or stylized versions of it. A significant example is a clay sealing from the early pillar basement at Knossos (H.M. 159). This is a clay impression (sealing) made by a seal stone and is among the earliest in date of such sealings found in Crete. (Fig. 12) It features three pictographs, symbols which appear to have developed into the as yet undeciphered Minoan hieroglyphs. The pictographs represent a man's leg, a simplified double axe, and a fish. The simplified double axe has the shape of a cross between two curved verticals, i.e, the two blade edges. If we compare this with a clay sealing from the Temple Repository at Knossos (H.M. 152), we find that the cross between the curved vertical horns of the bull here represented makes a pattern closely approaching the shape of a double axe and appearing where a double axe is frequently placed, between the bull's horns. (Fig. 13) I have seen another similar sealing in the Heraclion Museum (Gallery IX, Case 124). The sealing, which is unnumbered, comes from Zakros and is dated Middle Minoan III A to Late Minoan I (c. 1700-1450 B.C.). This sealing also displays a bull's head with horns rising vertically to frame a simplified X-type of cross.[12] (Fig. 14)

An interesting circular seal throws light on this problem. It is a Late Minoan gem from the Knossos district (A.M. 1938. 1070). The engraving shows a bull-man or Minotaur arched back in a circular fashion so that his human legs nearly touch his horned bull's head. Although the upper part of the body is clearly that of a bull, the horns have been rendered figuratively rather than naturalistically. One horn has become two-pronged while the other is in the shape of an eight-rayed sun-disk. (Fig.

15) In keeping with the circular design is a curved bough with buds which arches beneath the belly of the Minotaur. We have, of course, no double axe here, but in the place of a double axe or of a crossed rectangle we find an eight-rayed sun-disk.

The inference to be drawn is that the double axe, the cross design within a rectangle, and an eight-rayed sun are in some sense equivalents. We have previously seen that the number eight is the sun-god's number. It is also the number of the sacred king or Minos who represents the god on earth and who is here suggested by the human legs of the Minotaur. The bough with buds is an obvious fertility symbol and is related to both god and king. Finally, the circular design of the whole composition suggests the sun's yearly cycle as well as the tanist motif in which lion chases bull and vice versa. It therefore appears that both the sun-god and the priest-king must pass between horns to enter the labrys or Labyrinth.

Now if the word "labyrinth" is derived from "labrys" (double axe) we should expect to find that the nature and shape of the Labyrinth should have something in common with the nature and shape of the double axe. An this is precisely what we do find. As we have seen, a simplified double axe between two upright members (horns) forms a pattern which is essentially a rectangle with two diagonals which make an inscribed cross. This very simple geometrical pattern occurs, sometimes with slight variations, on a great many Minoan seals and is frequently found on seals with several faces providing a context of presumably related symbols. Although it appears combined with a variety of motifs, it is often associated with bulls, spirals, and mazes. Now since the Minotaur was kept in the Labyrinth and the Labyrinth was some kind of maze, the combination of these motifs with the labrys-shaped pattern of a crossed rectangle appears significant. It suggests that the Labyrinth was a maze, shaped externally like a rectangle, and including as an essential feature crossed diagonals. In other words, it would be shaped like a double axe in a rectangular enclosure.

Let us look at some pictorial evidence, which supports this deduction. If we compare the seal designs illustrated in Figures

11, 13, 16, and 17, we can see the relationship between the labrys and the Labyrinth. (Fig. 18) All of these seal designs come from the Palace at Knossos or from nearby and they date from Middle Minoan III to Late Minoan. I am not suggesting that they represent an evolution of motifs in time, but rather that their proximity in time and place supports the conclusion that they are related. I have already discussed the bucranium designs of Figures 11 and 13. Figure 16 is a seal stone with two impression faces from the Heraclion Museum (Gallery II, Case 28, No. 1786). Face (a) is a simple rectangle with crossed diagonals and has small graduation marks dividing the rectangular border into equal segments or degrees. Face (b) contains a bull's head and a small three-petaled flower which is probably a lily, a flower sacred to the goddess. The sun-bull and lily of the goddess are here associated with an abstract design recalling the shape of the double axe. The seal in Figure 17 (H.M., Gallery V, Case 65, No. 2180) shows an interesting variation on the crossed rectangle design. Although it is not highly complex, it does suggest with economy a maze or labyrinth. There are four concentric rectangular tracks which, if we follow in circular sequence inward to the center, suggest a spiral, and the diagonals together with the diminishing vertical and horizontal members suggest a more complex way of spiralling inward and out again.

This example is not unique. In the Ashmolean Museum there are three seals which closely parallel this particular design.[13] All three are dated Late Minoan and, hence, are contemporary with the seal described above. It is also worth noting that two of these seals are white glass and one blue glass, colors symbolic of the goddess, and two of them were found in places of religious significance and were probably votive offerings. One was found in the famous sanctuary of the Dictaean Cave, which, as we have seen, was where the goddess Rhea raised the infant Zeus, and the other was found in a tholos tomb at Hagia Pelagia, which suggests that the emblem has some reference to death and the hereafter. But these observations anticipate a problem to be discussed later. At the moment, it is sufficient to point out that this design is not abstract art for art's sake, but an emblem of the mysterious Labyrinth, a symbol of central importance in the grand design of Minoan religion.

I have been referring above to a specific rendering of the labyrinth motif but in essence it is a quadrangle with crossed diagonals and the inventive Minoan artists conceived a multitude of variations on this basic pattern. My insistence that the pattern had its origin in religious iconography does not preclude the possibility, indeed the likelihood, that so well known a pattern could also be used quite casually as an ornamental design divorced from any religious intent. When variations on it appear, as they do, in borders on utilitarian pottery and the like, we may be reasonably certain that a religious significance is not consciously intended. But when it appears on talismanic gems, on votive offerings, or in other clearly religious contexts, we may reasonably conclude that it was used with deliberate symbolic intent.

A beautifully engraved gem from the Middle Minoan Period is in the latter category. It is a flattened cylinder seal of banded agate in the Ashmolean Collection (A.M. 1938. 964). The engraving pictures a bull, the ceremonial sport of bull-vaulting, and a labyrinth design. (Fig. 19a and b) The bull has his forelegs and head in a position which connotes his entry into the upper right-hand corner of the labyrinth, while over his head the acrobat is in the upswing of a vaulting somersault over the bull's body.

The design has been usually interpreted as a bull drinking at a cistern. But I believe that is an error which stems from an ignorance of the significance of the labyrinth motif. That we are dealing here with a variation on the labyrinth motif should be easy to recognize in the light of the examples previously discussed. It is a quadrangle with crossed diagonals and the variation is that this design is achieved by a lozenge-shaped meander. The meander pattern like the spiral connotes the complexity of the labyrinth as a maze. The bull is not drinking from a cistern decorated with a meaningless abstract design; he is symbolically entering the labyrinth in which he will meet his ritual death at the hands of the vaulting toreador whose dirk can be clearly seen, sheathed at his belt. It is well known from an abundance of representations that the bull-vaulting sport had ritual significance in connection with a calendric festival of some sort. And according to tradition the Minos-bull was kept in the Labyrinth. Certainly we are dealing here with this kind of symbolic relationship rather than with a naturalistic picture of a bull drinking. If the picture is naturalistic, it is strange that the acrobat should choose this moment to vault over the bull, a feat difficult enough at best without the obstruction of a large tank of water to be hurdled first.

Furthermore, there is other evidence that this is a labyrinth symbol and not a drinking trough. In a bay of the central court at the Palace at Phaistos there is a painted plaster fresco on a wall surface of considerable size which so closely resembles the labyrinth pattern on this seal that several scholars have been struck by the similarity.[14] The Phaistos fresco, which I photographed on the site, is not entirely complete or preserved but there is quite enough of it remaining to permit comparison with the seal. (Fig. 20) It is a simple quadrangle with crossed diagonals composed of a lattice meander outline in red. The lozenge-shaped meander is the same as that on the seal and the ratio of linear proportions is approximately the same also. The fresco does not decorate a lowly cistern for watering stock. On the contrary, it enjoys a position of apparent public importance since it is located in the great central court of the Royal Palace. It is dated Middle Minoan III b by Pendlebury, a period in which Knossos and Phaistos are known to have had close relations and also the period in which the similar seal was made. The remarkable similarity of the Phaistos fresco and the design on the seal stone was noted by James Walter Graham in his discussion of Phaistos in *The Palaces of Crete*. Graham also noticed that the central court at Phaistos, where the fresco stands in an alcove of the wall, shows clear traces that doors once protected all openings. He concludes that the doors existed to seal off the central court upon festival occasions when, he believes, the court was used as an arena for staging the bull games. He infers, rightly I think, that the engraver of the seal stone associated the fresco meander design with the bull games because it occupies such a conspicuous position in the arena where the games actually took place. He also writes that "it is quite possible that the pattern had some symbolical connection, presumably religious, with the bull games."[15] But he does not offer any explanation of what that "symbolical connection" might be.

In the light of this evidence, I believe that the seal stone provides the clue to the significance of the fresco at Phaistos. Both contain a labyrinth emblem which has reference to a calendric religious ceremony celebrated periodically by bull-vaulting games and a sacrifice to the great goddess at the Palace of Minos in Knossos and in the Palace of Rhadamanthus, his brother, at Phaistos.

Fragments of a fresco similar to the Phaistos labyrinth fresco were discovered at the Palace at Knossos and this fresco dates from the same period as the Phaistos fresco (Middle Minoan III). Pendlebury describes this fresco at Knossos as follows: "In the Loomweight Area, fallen from the hall above, were fragments of an elaborate spiral design apparently forming a square frame with two diagonals, a pattern recalling an M.M. III b painting of lattice-work at Phaistos. The background is a deep red and the spirals are blue picked out with black and white. Similar designs were found elsewhere in the Palace."[16] Pendlebury also adds that fragments of painted stucco relief, found in the same deposit, could be identified as representations of oxen and of a human arm and he infers that the fresco probably pictured a bull-grappling contest.

In view of all of the foregoing evidence, I conclude that the quadrangular motif with crossed diagonals is a symbol of the labyrinth. It has the shape of a double axe within an enclosure that frequently also suggests a maze and it is closely associated with the ritual bull-games. The labyrinth is quite literally the maze that encloses the labrys and contains the Minotaur.

NOTES

[1] R. F. Willetts, *Cretan Cults and Festivals* (New York, 1961), p. 75.

[2] For instance, in the Pythagorean system a pentad of five points $\therefore$ stood for the five elements—earth, air, fire, water, and the fifth essence or quintessence, spirit. Therefore, it was a symbol of ultimate substance. As ultimate substance, the number five would have been associated by the Minoans with the great goddess and consequently would have been considered a feminine number. The Pythagoreans, however, reversed the sexual significance of numbers making odd numbers male and even numbers female. Robert Graves, *The White Goddess* (New York, 1948), p. 196.

[3] Graves, *White Goddess*, p. 307.

[4] Graves, *White Goddess*, p. 305.

[5] Willetts, *Cretan Cults and Festivals*, pp. 252-255.

[6] Willetts, *Cretan Cults and Festivals*, p. 52. According to one myth Iasion embraced Demeter, who was a later type of the fertility goddess, in a thrice-ploughed field, that is, in a field prepared for sowing. Iasion, as well as the other Dactyls, clearly had phallic significance. Willetts, *Cretan Cults and Festivals*, p. 113.

[7] Graves, *White Goddess*, p. 305.

[8] Graves, *White Goddess*, p. 196.

[9] Emily Vermeule, *Greece in the Bronze Age* (Chicago and London, 1967), p. 293.

[10] Willetts, *Cretan Cults and Festivals*, p. 80.

[11] Willetts, *Cretan Cults and Festivals*, p. 82.

[12] It seems probable that the stag of St. Hubertus, a stag with a cross between his horns, is a later Christian adaptation of this

very ancient sacred motif. If this identification is correct, it probably stands for Christ as sun-king.

[13] The seals are illustrated in Kenna's catalogue and numbered as follows: No. 360 (A.M. 1941. 1240), No. 361 (A.E. 704), No. 362 (A.E. 1239 (c)). V. E. G. Kenna, *Cretan Seals* (Oxford, 1960).

[14] Rf. R. W. Hutchinson, *Prehistoric Crete* (London, 1962), p. 179 and V. E. G. Kenna, *Cretan Seals,* p. 118.

[15] James Walter Graham, *The Palaces of Crete* (Princeton, 1962), p. 79.

[16] J. D. S. Pendlebury, *The Archaeology of Crete* (New York, 1965), p. 156.

Chapter III

A BORDER INSPECTION

Homer tells us in a cryptic passage in the *Odyssey* that Minos of Knossos was "king for nine years, a familiar of mighty Zeus."[1] This passage has interested many scholars and it has been variously interpreted, but the commonly accepted interpretation has been that the Minoan kingship was governed by a lunar-solar cycle of eight years at the end of which the king had to renew his sacred powers by a ritual reunion with the god-head from which he emerged, as if, reborn.[2] This interpretation is based primarily on three grounds. (1) It is an astronomical fact that the solar year of 365 days is longer by 11 days than the lunar year of 354 days with the consequence that the start of the solar year can be made to coincide with the start of a lunar year at new moon in no shorter period than every eight years. This, of course, is only an approximate co-ordination, but it is easily observed without elaborate instruments and is a close enough reconciliation of lunar and solar time for ritual purposes. (2) Although Homer speaks of nine years, it was the ancient Greek practice to include both the first and last terms of a sequence in counting, so that nine years by his count would yield what we would call eight years. (3) The final ground for the interpretation is that periodic kingship, including the replacement or renewal of a sacred king at the end of a great year, is known to have been a practice common to many ancient cultures with a solar-lunar religious base.

In addition to Homer there is a good deal of evidence from other sources that the Minoan kings at Knossos ruled for eight year periods and underwent a ritual of renewal, if not actual replacement, at the expiration of this term.³ For instance, we may recall the myth of Theseus previously mentioned. Seven maids and seven youths were sent by the Athenians as tribute to Minos every eight years. It makes numerical and mythical sense to see in this account seven victims of each sex sacrificed yearly in place of the king, Minos himself being the lucky eighth who is ritually reborn at the end of the lunar-solar cycle. By putting together these hints and others from additional sources it has seemed reasonable to infer that the Minoan kingship must have been regulated by a solar-lunar calendar based on an eight year cycle. But so far as I am aware, it has always been assumed that no such calendar in graphic form has survived or that, at least, none has as yet been found or recognized.

I shall attempt to show that such a calendar does exist in a fragmentary state of preservation but sufficiently complete to be recognized for what it is and read and interpreted with reasonably accuracy. I believe that when the evidence I shall present is fully examined, it will be apparent that the well known Toreador Fresco from Knossos has concealed in its border design a most ingenious and surprisingly accurate ritual calendar.

Like all of the frescoes discovered at Knossos, the Toreador Fresco was found in fragments and put together like a jig-saw puzzle. Fortunately, enough pieces were discovered to make a tolerably accurate and complete reconstruction possible. There is no doubt about the general configuration of its central picture, three toreadors and a charging bull, nor about the general features of its border design. (See Plate I) The existing pieces are, for the most part, so widely distributed over the design as a whole that the gaps can be easily conjectured and filled by continuing lines and patterns consistently with the extant remains. But as is always true in restorations of this kind, it is possible to over-restore in the interest of aesthetic effect or mis-restore in the interest of leaving undisturbed existing fragments that have become obviously warped from their original position by cracking, contracting, or swelling. These considerations appear to have brought about three different restorations of the fresco. At any rate, three versions exist and each has merit in its own way.

The original fragments are arranged in a version which is housed in the Heraclion Museum (Gallery XIV). Although this version contains the extant fragments themselves upon the basis of which all three versions ultimately rest, it is not the most reliable version in respect to the parts that have been added to fill in the design nor even in regard to the fitting together of the existing fragments. (See Plate III) I have carefully studied this version in the Heraclion Museum and have diagrammed its differences from the other two versions. The fact is that this version is the end result of a laudable attempt to preserve the existing fragments which have endured rehousing, three earthquakes, and the havoc of the German occupation in World War II.[4] It is therefore not surprising that as a restoration it is not the most reliable version despite the authenticity of its fragments.

The version which is aesthetically most pleasing is the one which Evans published as an illustration in his *Palace of Minos*. In this version, the artist, E. Gillieron, who, under Evans' direction, was responsible for the color and draughtmanship of the restoration, has admirably caught the spirit of the original as suggested by the fragments, but it is not a meticulously accurate version in details, the artist having taken liberties in the direction of over-restoration and also of omission, particularly in the border design. (See Plate I) Evans was apparently dissatisfied with the archaeological accuracy of this version. He made careful notations, comments, and corrections on the proof copy of it, and this corrected proof became the basis for a later version which is less fully restored as well as much more sensitive and accurate. This second version has the restored areas of the border merely indicated in outline. It differs from the first version in many details and most notably in adhering strictly to the archaeological evidence of the fragments of the border design which had been treated rather impressionistically in the earlier version. This second version was not published until 1967 when it appeared for the first time in the *Knossos Fresco Atlas,* edited by Mark Cameron and Sinclair Hood. There it appears in an accurate color reproduction on a scale of about one half the size of the original fresco and numbered Plate IX, Second Version. This is unquestionably the most accurate reconstruction of the fragments of the fresco that once adorned the walls of the Palace at Knossos. (See Plate II)

I have used this version as my primary source supplemented by a study of the existing fragments as they appear restored in the Heraclion Museum reconstruction. An additional primary source of importance is the proof copy of Gillieron's first version containing the pencilled notes of Evans which lie behind the changes made in the second more accurate version. Fortunately, I have had an opportunity to study this proof in the archives of the Ashmolean Museum at Oxford and to record the directions for revision which Evans pencilled on it. A number of these comments were quite pertinent in providing a basis for a truly accurate reconstruction of the border design. Since the entire mathematical aspect of the calendar, and most of its symbolic import as well, lies concealed in the border, it is highly important to work from a version of this design which has not been tampered with or treated carelessly in ignorance of its significance.

Although Evans showed concern to achieve a reconstruction of the border design which faithfully followed his archaelogical evidence, he did not suspect that the border was anything other than merely decorative. In fact, he interpreted the border motif as stylized rocks by analogy with certain other fresco borders and architectural dados with sequences of variegated square panels that clearly do imitate polished marble or veined stone surfaces.[5] However, the Toreador Fresco border is actually very different from these square paneled dados with their irregular and unsystematic vein markings. By contrast the running border panels are crescent-shaped rather than square, their "veins" are regular and symmetrical, and the series of panels runs through five variations in color and then repeats this sequence with ordered regularity.

There are other design motifs in Minoan art which closely parallel these features. Let us look at them and see in what context they occur. One is an ivory seal from a tholos tomb at Platanos in the Messara (H.M. 1044) dated Early Minoan to Middle Minoan I. It is skillfully carved in the shape of a bull-calf and it is pierced with two holes so that it may be worn on a cord suspended from the neck. It was probably an amulet worn for its magical quality. (Fig. 21) The impression face is engraved with a design which is similar to certain aspects of the Toreador Fresco. Within a rectangular border are two animals. The animal on the left has longer legs than the other and a protrusion at the head which suggests horns. It is, therefore, probably a bull. The animal on the right is smaller, hornless, and its head is feline. It appears to be a lion. The combination of the two is a variation on the bull-lion motif previously discussed. As we have seen, this motif has calendric significance, the two animals being calendar beasts of the bi-partite year. Below the two beasts are two crescent moons facing in opposite directions representing the first and last phases of the moon. But the most interesting feature is the border. It maintains the moon motif in a running sequence of crescents framing the rectangular picture much as the crescents of the fresco border frame the Toreadors. Moreover, the convex curves of the crescents on both horizontal borders face in the same direction as the corresponding crescents on the fresco border. The crescents on the vertical borders alternate in direction. There are 18 crescents in all, 6 on each horizontal border and 3 on each vertical border.

The evidence may be put together as follows. The seal is obviously related to a religious context. It was found in a tomb and was worn as a protective amulet. It is carved in the shape of a bull, sacred beast of the sun-god, from white ivory in honor of the moon-goddess. The bull and lion on the engravings are calendar beasts of the solar year and they are associated with lunar symbols in sequence within the field and on the border. The significance of the seal is therefore not only religious but specifically calendric and its border is suggestively like that of the Toreador Fresco.

Let us look at another seal from the same area and of the same period. It was also found in a tholos tomb in the Messara at Kalathiana (H.M. 821). This seal is also carved from white ivory, but it is in the shape of a crouching lion. (Fig. 22) It, too, has holes for a cord and was probably another amulet. It is engraved with an abstract design featuring five curved members in a running sequence. A fragment of the seal is missing, but there can be no doubt that the sequence contains exactly five members. We may now recall that the design on the border of the Toreador Fresco is arranged in regular sequences of five members of differing colors. The shape of the members on the seal design is not literally a crescent, but it could well be a stylized variation on a crescent motif. It is associated with white, the moon-goddess' color, the number five, a number sacred to the goddess, and a calendar beast, the lion, and it was found in a religious context and used as an amulet. The sequence of five members, then, might very well be interpreted as five phases of the moon.

Using these parallels with the fresco border as clues, let us look more closely at the sequence of five crescent-shaped members. It makes symbolic sense to read these as five phases of the moon in the course of one complete lunation. Starting in the lower left corner of the border and working up the vertical pillar, we find that the first symbol is orange and marked with wavy lines at the crescent end and with little crescents in the center. If this is a symbol for the new moon, as the small crescents suggest, then we should expect it to be preceded by a dark symbol representing the brief period each month when the moon is not visible at all in the night sky. And that is what we do find. The second symbol is black like the sky on a moonless night but dotted with tiny white and red points like stars. It is true that moonless nights provide the best conditions for viewing the stars.

The third symbol is blue and marked with wavy lines throughout. We must move to the top of the vertical border to see a preserved example. This should be a symbol of the waxing moon. It is a blue moon, a virgin moon. Blue, incidentally, is the color of the Virgin Mary even in Christian symbolism.

We must move to the upper horizontal border to find a preserved example of the fourth symbol. It follows the blue symbol when moving from right to left. The fourth symbol is white and marked with small crescents. White as well as blue are colors usually associated with the moon-goddess, but white is her principal color. This should be a symbol, then, of her central phase, the mature, luminous, white full moon—marked perhaps by a few visible craters.

The fifth symbol is red and marked with wavy lines. The wavy lines bend gracefully in both directions. This is true of the blue symbols as well. I take this to mean we may read the sequence of symbols in either direction. The sequence maintains its integrity, but we must begin a phase with the opposite end of each symbol and adjacent symbols exchange significance. The primary significance of the red symbol is, accordingly, the waning phase of the old moon, but when reading from the opposite direction it becomes a symbol of the new moon since it is adjacent to the orange symbol.

The primary significance of the five symbols, then, is as follows. (1) Orange, new moon. (2) Blue, waxing moon. (3) White, full moon. (4) Red, waning moon. (5) Black, moonless sky. But since they may be read in either direction, a line tangent to either the convex or the concave margin of the symbol will represent the point of transition from one phase to the next. Consequently symbols may maintain their primary significance as indicators of this point of transition regardless of the direction in which they are read. However, for the duration of the phase which follows, adjacent symbols will exchange significance depending upon the direction in which they are read.

Orange is the new moon symbol and the first of the sequence. A line tangent to either its convex or concave crescent will indicate the first visible new moon of a lunation. But since it may be read in either direction from either of these points, the two phase symbols adjacent on either side may represent the period immediately following the first appearance of a new moon. Therefore, either the black or the red symbol may represent this period depending upon the direction of reading. And the orange symbol itself may represent the duration of the period preceding the first appearance of a new moon since both its crescent margins may indicate the point of transition. The remaining two symbols, the white and the blue, never begin or end the sequence. Depending upon the direction of reading, they will represent either the waxing moon or the full moon. And since the mid point in a sequence of five symbols will represent the single night of absolute full moon, the middle of either the white or the blue symbol will signify this point. Now we have seen a complete sequence of the five symbols, and we have discovered that they may be read in either direction.

Since a lunar year consists of twelve lunations, we should expect to find 12 x 5 or 60 moon phase symbols in all. But a count gives us 23 in each horizontal border and 8 in each vertical border for a total of 62. However, at this point we may notice that the border is not truly symmetrical, as would be appropriate if it were merely a decorative element of the fresco. The horizontal elements of the border extend beyond the vertical elements like a threshold below and a lintel above a doorway with two vertical pillars. Peculiarly, the right-hand ends of the horizontals extend farther beyond the verticals than the left-hand ends. And on the right-hand ends, exactly one moon phase extends beyond the verticals, whereas on the left-hand ends, the moon phase ends neatly at the margin of the verticals although the track-like marks bordering the moon symbols continue. We may also note that both the extending moon symbols of the horizontal borders are orange new moon symbols. Their counterparts are the two orange new moon symbols which begin each vertical sequence at the bottom of each pillar.

In short, we have a deliberate arrangement of parallel or overlapping symbols at the ends of the verticals and the ends of the horizontals. If in reading a sequence we should turn a corner where this overlapping occurs, we would naturally count only one of the two parallel new moon symbols to maintain a correct sequence. But if this is so, then we have two new moon symbols that we have not actually counted in making a circuit of the border. Hence, we would use in all 60 phase symbols rather than the 62 available. The conclusion is that the 60 phases we have counted represent a lunar year of 12 x 5 phases.

If this conclusion is sound, we should be able to read the 60 phases of a lunar year in a way which maintains a proper sequence of phase symbols for each of 12 lunations. The possible ways of doing this successfully are limited by the fact that overlapping symbols of the same phase in different borders permit certain junctions to be made while excluding others. The base of each vertical border ends with an orange symbol and the top of each ends with a blue symbol. The right-hand end of each horizontal border ends with an orange symbol and the left-hand end of each ends with a blue symbol.

As we have seen, the symbols may be read in either direction. Let us begin with the orange new moon symbol at the base of the left vertical border. If we begin at a line tangent to the convex margin of this symbol, considering this point to represent the new moon, and count upward five full phases, we arrive at a point where again a line may be drawn tangent to the convex margin of the following orange symbol. This represents one complete lunation from new moon to new moon.

Continuing upward two more phases brings us to a blue symbol at the top of the vertical border. But since the left-hand end of the top border begins with a blue symbol, we can make a junction which will maintain the proper sequence. The junction will also involve a change of direction in reading the symbols. The first blue symbol at the top border will, accordingly, be full moon and a count of five full phases will take us to the concave margin of the orange new moon symbol. The course of five symbols represents a second full lunation. Working from left to right across the top border, we find four more complete sequences of five symbols each. This gives us a total of six complete lunations or half of a lunar year.

We may now drop to the right hand end of the bottom border and make a junction because the orange symbol ends the top border and begins the bottom border. This will again involve a change in direction of reading. And since this is so, the right margin of the upper symbol will correspond with the left margin of the lower symbol. We are also beginning a sequence of five, so we may count one of these orange symbols but not both. Let us consider the convex margin of the lower orange symbol as the first appearance of new moon. Then counting from right to left along the bottom border we find four sequences of five symbols each which brings us to a point two symbols short of the end of the border. The count to this point is ten complete lunations.

Next we must move diagonally across the fresco to the top of the right vertical border which is the only border we have not used. Again a junction is possible because a blue symbol may be joined with its like. Once more we must change the direction of reading. But since we are not at the beginning of a sequence, we must count both blue symbols. The first is a waxing moon, the second a full moon. A count of five symbols brings us to the concave margin of the orange new moon symbol. This is the eleventh lunation.

If we count down five more symbols, we arrive at the concave margin of the last orange symbol, which again represents a complete lunation. This is the twelfth lunation, completing a lunar year, and making use of all 60 symbols and the entire border. It is apparent, then, that the border of the fresco represents twelve lunations in sequences of five phases each and that they may be read in a way that maintains the proper order of the five phases.

The next step is to take a look at a feature of the border which we have thus far ignored. There are four parallel tracks, two blue and two orange, on the external edges of the border and following the moon symbols around it. They are marked with lines more or less evenly spaced like degrees. Although there are many more marks here, they recall the graduations on the rectangular border of the labyrinth motif we have previously observed on an engraved seal. (Fig. 16, a) The fresco, of course, is also basically a rectangle and it contains a representation of bullvaulting in its center—a motif which we have seen is associated with the labyrinth design. It seems likely, then, that the fresco may also be a labyrinth as well as a calendar, but we have yet to discover a way through its maze.

Since the four tracks are blue and orange, we may suspect that the orange may have reference to the sun, for that is the sun's color. The blue would then be a reference to the moon, for that is one of her colors. A solar-lunar calendar must reconcile the yearly progress of the sun with the phases of the moon. The four tracks marked with graduations might well be day indicators by this logic. If we compare a few of the moon symbols with the track marks parallelling them, we discover that although the count is not always precisely the same it approximates six marks per phase. We have 60 such phases to be actually used in a circuit of the border. Now 60 x 6 gives us 360 which is only five short of the number of days in a solar year. And if there are five phases in a lunation and approximately six marks per phase, we would have 5 x 6 or 30 marks per lunation which is close to the 29.5 days of an average lunation or lunar month. Of course these rough correlations are not close enough to be useful as anything more than a clue. Yet it does appear that the four graduated tracks should be read as days.

But why should there be four tracks? It is obvious that the four tracks are not the same. They differ in color and the day marks on parallel blue and orange tracks do not coincide. We may now recall that much evidence suggests that the Minoan kingship was governed by an eight year period or great year. This is the shortest period in which solar and lunar time can be reconciled. That is to say every eight years a solar year beginning at the solstice will coincide with the beginning of a lunation and make it possible to begin reckoning solar and lunar time together. The natural conclusion is that the four tracks represent four years or half of such an eight year cycle.

We have now observed a number of symbolic references which tie in with each other and also with some rough mathematical correspondences to astronomical facts concerning the sun and the moon. We are apparently dealing with intentional solar and lunar symbolism. In the light of the evidence examined thus far, it is difficult to believe that the border of this fresco was intended to be a stylized decoration representing rocks. But the significance of the apparent astronomical correspondences is not yet clear. If the fresco border is a calendar, we should be able to read it, and it should be astronomically accurate. The question is how to read it. But that is to anticipate the subject of the next chapter.

NOTES

[1] *Odyssey,* Book XIX.
[2] Sir James George Frazer, *The New Golden Bough* (New York, 1968), p. 234. And Willetts, *Cretan Cults and Festivals,* pp. 94-95.
[3] Willetts, *Cretan Cults and Festivals,* pp. 92-99.
[4] See Appendix for a more detailed discussion.
[5] Sir Arthur Evans, *The Palace of Minos,* 7 vol. (London, 1930), Vol. III, p. 211; Vol. IV, pp. 892-894.

Chapter IV

THREADING THE LABYRINTH

As we know from myth, the Labyrinth is a dangerous maze to enter. Many who entered it never returned. One who did return was the hero, Theseus. But he had the help of the goddess in the person of fair-haired Ariadne. She gave Theseus a ball of thread and tied one end to a pillar at the entrance of the Labyrinth. He entered the maze at the pillar and unwound the thread as he went. He found the Minotaur in the center, slew him, and followed the thread back to Ariadne.

If we are to enter the Labyrinth and find our way back again, we shall need the help of the goddess. And if we are to stand in her grace, we had better treat with respect her mythopoeic mode of thought. If we do so, she may provide us with a thread of poetically connected associations that, perhaps, will guide us to the center of the maze and lead us safely out again. But I do not think she will be offended if we also take with us an accurate map and some tools of analytic logic which we will need as well from time to time.

The map is the first problem. The fresco is in fragments and it is necessary to construct from those fragments as accurate a picture of the border as is possible. Evans' Second Version restoration (Plate II) provides the basis for such a reconstruction. The restoration by itself will not serve the purpose because no attempt has been made to supply marks on the day tracks of the bottom border where they are missing. Furthermore, the day tracks which have been restored on the other three borders, where pieces of the fresco are missing, are conjectural anyway. They were filled in by analogy with the existing marks on the extant fragments and they are, therefore, probably only approximately accurate although certainly more nearly accurate than the restored marks on the other two fresco reconstructions.

But there is no way of knowing what criterion was used—other than an artist's eye for symmetry—in filling them in. Therefore, it makes good sense to provide a check upon them by constructing a model of the border arrived at by a systematic application of measurement and proportional ratios derived from the existing fragments only. This is what I have done.

My method of procedure was as follows. First an accurate draft was made of the existing fragments only, using Evans' Second Version as a basis. A study of the fragment joints and Evans' notes on the Ashmolean proof of the first version proved that the proportions of the border in relation to the picture which they frame could not be extended or contracted in a horizontal direction without doing violence to the evidence provided by the extant fragments. On the other hand, slight extension or slight contraction of the vertical borders is hypothetically possible. However, the vertical proportions of the central picture and fragments joining elements of the picture with elements of the border admit only a very small tolerance for possible error here.[1] My conclusion was that the proportions of the border established by Evans' Second Version are as nearly accurate as they can be made and sufficiently reliable to provide a basis for analysis.

The next step was to take as many samples as possible from each of the four day tracks in each of the four border members. Samples of given magnitudes from existing fragments provided a basis for determining the average number of day marks per inch on each of the sixteen tracks. Then it was possible to calculate the number of day marks to be added on each of sixteen tracks wherever existing fragments did not provide them. This procedure provided the basis for the diagramatic reconstruction of the border illustrated in Plate IV.[2]

A count of the day marks thus derived yielded interesting results. A summary of these results is diagramed in Figure 23. The number of marks in the blue tracks differed from the number in the orange tracks on each of the four borders. And the number of marks on the tracks of the upper horizontal border differed significantly from the number on the corresponding tracks of the lower border. But the differences were consistently in intervals of ten marks. A correlation with this interval appeared in the 7 + 3 or 10 marks in the areas of the horizontal borders which extended beyond the vertical borders. As we have previously seen, these are the areas where there is either no moon symbol or an overlap in moon symbols. Presumably these areas, as well as the corresponding overlap areas at the bottom of both vertical borders, call for an adjustment of some sort in the count of total day marks in a circuit of the border.

But in what fashion should we make such a circuit? We have seen in Chapter III how a circuit of the border may be made so that the 60 moon symbols maintain a proper sequence. If solar and lunar time are to be kept in pace, this sequence, or one like it, will have to be observed. But it would be possible to start the lunar sequence at any new moon symbol, and it would also be possible to reverse the sequence as we have seen. The question is where should we start and in what order should we use the 16 available day tracks.

A rather surprising departure from aesthetic symmetry provides a clue. The top border presents a different color sequence from the other three borders. (See Plate II) Reading from the inside to the outside, the color sequence of the day tracks on three borders is orange, blue, blue, orange. But on the top border alone the sequence is orange, blue, orange, blue. Orange is the sun's color and blue is one of the moon's colors. In a solar-lunar calendar the sun and the moon should march together—or perhaps dance together. As an experiment, let us assume this is a clue.

Let us start at the lower left corner of the border and tie our thread to the vertical pillar, which I take to be the entrance to the Labyrinth where Ariadne tied the thread for Theseus. There are good reasons for choosing this as the entrance. First, because it allows us to begin the lunar year with a new moon symbol. And secondly, because it is known that the Linear B script, examples of which were found at Knossos, is read from left to right.

If we begin on the outside orange track and count upward, we get a count of 51 days in the vertical pillar. Now if we move to the top border and follow our color clue, we should use a blue track after having used an orange one, since the sequence should be orange, blue, orange, blue. Let us omit the first three marks because there is no moon symbol parallel to them and they represent an overlap. Then counting from left to right and again omitting the overlap at the end, we get a total of 140 days. The overlap indicates that we must now drop to the bottom right-hand corner of the border and move from right to left along it. Our color clue demands that we use the orange track next. Let us use the outside orange track, omitting again the overlap area of seven marks. Counting from right to left and once more omitting the overlap area of three marks at the far end, we get 130 days. There now remains only one border we have not used. It is the right-hand vertical border. The moon symbols indicate that we must begin at the top of this border and count downward. The proper track this time is blue. If we count downward from the outside blue track, omitting the last five marks—an overlap again—we get 44 days.

Now let us total our results. The figures are $51 + 140 + 130 + 44$ which equals 365 days or one solar year.

We have spiralled into the Labyrinth and in doing so we have been obliged to make a diagonal crossing from the lower left corner of the rectangle to the upper right corner. But shouldn't we have expected this anyway? The labyrinth motif, as we have seen, calls for a double axe within its enclosure, i.e., two diagonals inscribed in a rectangle. We have already made one such crossing. Following poetic logic, we should spiral back and make another one. We have used only four tracks of an available sixteen. And since we have reason to expect to find an eight year solar-lunar cycle, it behooves us to explore the remaining tracks.

At this point it will be more convenient to use the diagram in Figure 23. There it will be seen that the tracks are labeled to indicate their color, the order in which they should be used in a course of four years, the overlap areas to be omitted, the number of days in each track, and the direction in which to move about the border in each of four years.

Year 1 ends on the right on a blue track. Year 2 begins on the right on the outside orange track. The color sequence already established is maintained for two years and then is reversed in years 3 and 4. As it has been shown, there is a five day overlap at the lower end of both vertical borders. Since years begin alternately at these two points, it is necessary to omit either the first five marks or the last five. Mathematically it makes no difference which five one chooses to omit. But it appears symbolically appropriate to always omit the first five marks in every year so that it may be possible to begin each year on the margin of the new moon symbol which borders on the black symbol. But this, of course, is debatable since the symbols are read in either direction. In year 2 the course is up the right-hand border, then from left to right on the top border, then from right to left on the bottom border, and finally from top to bottom on the left-hand border. This order is demanded to maintain proper moon phase sequences, the proper number of days in seasons, and—as it will be shown later—the proper timing of ritual festivals. The day count is 46 + 140 + 130 + 49 or 365 days.

The pattern of movement in year 1, which began at the left, was basically a spiral with a diagonal crossing from lower left to upper right. In year 2, which began at the right, the pattern was serpentine rather than spiral. A diagonal crossing from corner to corner does not literally occur, but the jump made from the bottom of the horizontal border to the top of the left vertical border implies something analogous. The labyrinth motif is maintained, but by variation it has become more complex. In the years which begin on the left (years 1 and 3) the pattern is always spiral. Complementing this are the years which begin on the right (years 2 and 4) where the pattern is always serpentine. Since one and three are mystic numbers of the moon-goddess, it follows that the spiral pattern is her dance. And since two and four are sacred to the sun-god, the serpentine pattern must be his dance. The serpents so frequently associated with the goddess in works of art, then, are apparently sun-serpents and fundamentally phallic.

Year 3 begins at the left, and since the color sequence now reverses, it begins on the inner blue track. The pattern of movement is spiral as in year 1, but there is a significant variation in the day count. The total number of days is increased by one, and there is also a difference in distribution. The count is $44 + 150 + 120 + 52$ or 366 days. The additional day in the right-hand vertical track makes this a leap year. The other significant difference is that the upper border has gained ten days while the lower border has lost ten. We shall see later that this variation is explicable in terms of seasonal festivals.

Year 4 begins at the right on the inner blue track. As in year 2 the pattern is serpentine. The year ends at the left on the inside orange track, which is the innermost track of all. At this point we have used all sixteen tracks in a four year period and we have arrived at the innermost track and at the corner of the Labyrinth where we entered. The day count is $44 + 150 + 120 + 51$ or 365 days. We have obviously completed a four year cycle of the calendar and we are in position to start all over again.

It is apparent, then, how a cycle of four solar years may be reckoned on the day tracks. But what about lunar years? A lunar year of twelve lunations is approximately 354 days or 11 days short of the 365 days of a solar year. As we have seen, the crescent shaped margin of the orange new moon symbol coincides with the starting point of solar year 1 at a position five marks up from the bottom of the track. The symbolism indicates that a lunar year should be reckoned as beginning with a new moon rather than with a full moon or some other phase. It would be appropriate to begin reckoning a solar year at the winter solstice, since this—the shortest day of the year—is when the sun-god is, poetically speaking, reborn. It would, of course, be possible to begin reckoning a solar year from the summer solstice or from either of the equinoxes. However, as it will later be shown, the seasonal correspondences of the calendar indicate that we should begin a solar year at the winter solstice. Let us assume, then, that we may begin reckoning solar-lunar time from the winter solstice in a year in which this coincides with a new moon. The sun-god and the moon-goddess must begin their dance together.

As we have seen, there are 60 moon phase symbols to be traversed in a yearly circuit of the calendar. That is 12 lunations of 5 phases each. But since a solar year is 11 days longer than a lunar year, it is evident that while the sun-god and moon-goddess may begin their dance together, they can not end together in the course of a single year. It is also evident that the stationary moon symbols on the calendar, while they may indicate the proper sequence of moon phases and the number of lunations in a year, can not be made to literally coincide with the appearance of the moon in the night sky except at certain periodic intervals. The sun-god and the moon-goddess dance together in the sense that they part and rejoin in a complex, but nevertheless regular cyclical pattern.

The moon symbol at which we arrive at the end of solar year 1 is new moon. But the end of the twelfth lunation and beginning of the thirteenth lunation at a visible new moon will have occurred 11 days before. At the end of solar year 2 this discrepancy will be 22 days and at the end of year 3 it will be 33 days plus an additional day for leap year for a total of 34 days. But since an average lunation is approximately 29.5 days it will be possible to intercalate a thirteenth month here so that solar year 4 and a new lunar year may be begun approximately, although not perfectly, together. The discrepancy would be 4 days. The calendar indicates symbolically that the intercalation of a thirteenth month should be made by the spacing of the moon symbols in relation to the number of day marks in the right hand orange track which ends year 3. If we count ahead 30 days from the end of the twelfth lunation, we arrive at the new moon symbol which begins and ends each year on the calendar. Furthermore, as it will later be shown, the 4 day discrepancy would occur during a 5 day festival that marks the end of every solar year. The solar and lunar deities have been brought together again after 3 years by means of an extra month and a 5 day festival.

We begin year 4, then, with a 4 day discrepancy in the correlation of solar and lunar time. At the end of year 6, which of course is to enter a second 4 year cycle, the discrepancy will have increased to 37 days. The accumulation will include 4 days + 33 days in 3 years for a total of 37 days. Here, again the intercalation of a thirteenth 30 day month brings the start of solar and lunar years closer together. The discrepancy this time is 7 days.

However, at the end of year 8, which is also the end of the second 4 year cycle, a perfect correlation of solar-lunar time is achieved. The discrepancy of 7 days at the end of year 6 is increased by 22 days in 2 years and by 1 day in leap year (year 7). The result is 7 + 22 + 1 or 30 days. An intercalation of a thirteenth 30 day month absorbs these days exactly. And if we have been following lunar time on the calendar by counting on the day tracks used for the solar years, we will find that 30 more days in track 4 bring us to the new moon symbol at the end of the solar year. We may therefore begin a new 8 year cycle at new moon and winter solstice with the calendar calibrated to the astronomical facts.

The next problem is to discover how months should be counted in terms of days. The moon symbols on the calendar cannot be used for this purpose. The length of a lunation (5 moon symbols) in terms of day marks naturally varies with different tracks according to color and according to whether it is on a vertical border or either of the horizontal borders. The variation is from 34 day marks per lunation to 27 day marks per lunation, a maximum variation of 7 days.

Actual lunations, however, vary in length from approximately 29 days and 6 hours to 29 days and 20 hours. An average lunar month is 29 days, 12 hours, 44 minutes and 2 seconds or a little more than 29.5 days. What is significant about the moon symbols is that there are 12 lunations represented and 5 phases in each lunation. Accordingly we can infer that a normal lunar year was divided into 12 months and each month into 5 parts. The distribution of the 60 moon phase symbols over a 365 day solar year was made, as it has been shown, to indicate the times of cyclical correlation of the sun and moon, not as a means of counting a particular lunar month in days. But the kind of correlation achieved provides a basis for inferring how an official calendar month was probably counted in terms of days.

The later practice of the Greeks is also a clue, since there is good reason to believe that the calendars used in classical times had their roots in the Minoan calendar. The Greek practice was to count months alternately as 30 days and 29 days in length.[3] This method keeps calendar months close to the 29.5 days of an average lunation.

Let us experimentally apply this method to the calendar to see if it correlates. If we begin an 8 year cycle with a 30 day month and alternate with 29 day months to the end of year 3, we will end this year with a thirteenth 30 day month which is to be intercalated. Now if we begin year 4 with a 30 day month, as we have begun the previous years, we will have two 30 day months back to back.

Let us proceed to the end of year 6 alternating the lengths of the months. The intercalated thirteenth month at the end of this year is a 30 day month. Therefore, beginning year 7 with a 30 day month will again give us two long months in succession. The process is, of course, repeated once more at the end of year 8 when a 30 day month is intercalated at the end. The next 8 year cycle will begin with a 30 day month following a 30 day month.

In attempting to adjust this method to the calendar's 3 intercalated months in a way that is consistent and regular, we have been led to include 3 extra days in 8 years by putting 30 day months back to back. Had we maintained a simple 30 day, 29 day alternation throughout the 8 years despite the 3 intercalated months, we would wind up 3 days short of where the calendar ends its 8 year cycle. Clearly the calendar's structure demands the month lengths we have adopted if it is to work properly.

What is the significance of this month arrangement? As we have seen, 29.5 days is only an approximation of an actual average lunation. Expressed decimally an average lunation is more nearly 29.53 days. The calendar's 8 year cycle coincides with 99 lunations. In 99 lunations the .03 day fraction omitted in a crude reckoning based on a 29.5 day month will have accumulated a significant 2.97 day discrepancy or, for practical purposes, 3 days. The calendar has been designed with an accuracy which avoids this discrepancy by accommodating 3 extra days in the 3 intercalated months. Whoever designed the calendar was aware that an average lunation was longer than 29.5 days by about 45 minutes. Whether this knowledge was gained by careful observation and calculation, or by a lucky intuition in a process of trial and error, it is impossible to be sure. At any rate, when the calendar indicates that a new 8 year cycle is to begin at new moon on the winter solstice, the observable facts—the shortest day of the year and a new moon in the sky—will not contradict it to any very considerable degree. There will still be a small error—at maximum about a day and a half—because 99 lunations do not perfectly coincide with 8 solar years. This is not the fault of the calendar, but of the astronomical cycle itself which is not an absolute correlation.

We have now had a sightseeing tour in the labyrinth of the calendar, and thanks to Ariadne's thread, we have found our way through its spiral and serpentine eight year course to emerge at the base of the very pillar where we entered. We have seen how the sun and the moon dance together, parting at intervals but joining hands, as it were, at the end of the third, sixth, and eighth years. And we have also seen, although not yet fully, that they dance to the tune of myth. The mythic dance has its source in religious ritual and Minoan ritual was governed by calendric festivals. The festivals in turn have their roots in the seasons. The next step is to explore the calendar to see what it may tell us of festivals and seasons.

NOTES

[1] See detailed discussion in the Appendix.
[2] See Figure 41 in the Appendix for a Table showing how these results were derived from measurements.
[3] Willetts, *Cretan Cults and Festivals,* p. 93.

CHAPTER V

THE SEASONS OF THE SUN
AND THE FESTIVALS OF THE MOON

The rocky island of Crete warmed by the winds and waves of the Aegean and Libyan Seas enjoys a mild, almost semi-tropical climate for the larger part of every year. The windy peaks of Mount Ida, Mount Dicte and their like are whitened with snow in the coolest season, but the fertile plains like the Messara yield bountiful crops of olives, grapes and citrus fruits from sunny orchards and vineyards free of frost.

The Cretan seasons are really only three. Spring begins in early February. My first view of the Cretan countryside was in the first week of February and everywhere the farmers were engaged in spring chores. At Knossos on the very edges of the ruins of the Palace of Minos, the men in the vineyards carefully cultivated the soil about the roots of the grapes—soil which had hardened and crusted from a winter of lying fallow. And in the Messara near Phaistos, men and women pruned the silvery green boughs of the olive trees—a routine spring activity. Winter wheat was a hand high and lush green in the fields and all about were the natural signs of spring—pink almond blossoms, red and white anemones, asphodel, and yellow oxalis in colorful profusion.

The spring season, which is long and mild but not hot lasts until about the end of June when the long days of bright sun bring in the truly hot, dry weather of the summer season. The grain harvest comes in June and marks the end of spring. The seed grain is stored through the rainless summer and sowed again at the end of October. Grapes are harvested in September but the dry season lasts until late October or very early November. The trumpeting of the cranes flying south-east over Crete at this time in their biannual migration heralds the coming of fall. The farmers watch for this event for it means that the autumn rains are coming and it is time to begin fall ploughing and the sowing of grain crops.[1] This traditional sign of autumn in Crete and Greece is a bit of folk wisdom of very ancient origin. The migration of the cranes coincides roughly with the setting of the Pleiades in the morning sky, an event which Hesiod lays down as a rule for the beginning of fall ploughing. In Hesiod's time (c. 800 B.C.) the autumnal setting of the Pleiades fell on 26 October.[2]

The autumn and winter are really only one season in regard to weather and agricultural practice. The weather is cool but never really cold except at high altitudes and most of the heavy rainfalls of the entire year occur in this period.[3] The heaviest rains usually fall at the beginning and at the end of this period, marking it off from the rest of the year.[4] It is also the shortest season of the year lasting about 95 days or a little over three months.

The Cretan agricultural year is, therefore, a three season year much like the three season year of the Middle East. There is a long spring flight of about five months from February to the end of June. Then a shorter flight of about four months from July to late October. And a third short season of a little more than three months from late October through January.

With this seasonal pattern in mind, let us look at the calendar and test its correlation. We have reckoned solar-lunar time for 8 years from a starting point at winter solstice and new moon. If we begin year 1, then, on 21 December, omitting the first 5 marks, and count upward on the proper track 43 days, we arrive at a point 3 marks short of the end of the track. (See Figure 23) In counting solar years we have consistently omitted the first 3 marks at the left on the top horizontal tracks where no moon symbol occurs. Presumably these 3 marks ought to serve some purpose. I take them to signify that a 3 day festival marking the beginning of the spring season occurs at this time.

Plate I
The Toreador Fresco from Knossos. (c. 1500 B.C.) Sir Arthur Evans' first version of the restoration. Ashmolean Museum, Oxford.

Plate II
The Toreador Fresco from Knossos. (c. 1500 B.C.) Sir Arthur Evans' corrected version of the restoration. Ashmolean Museum, Oxford.

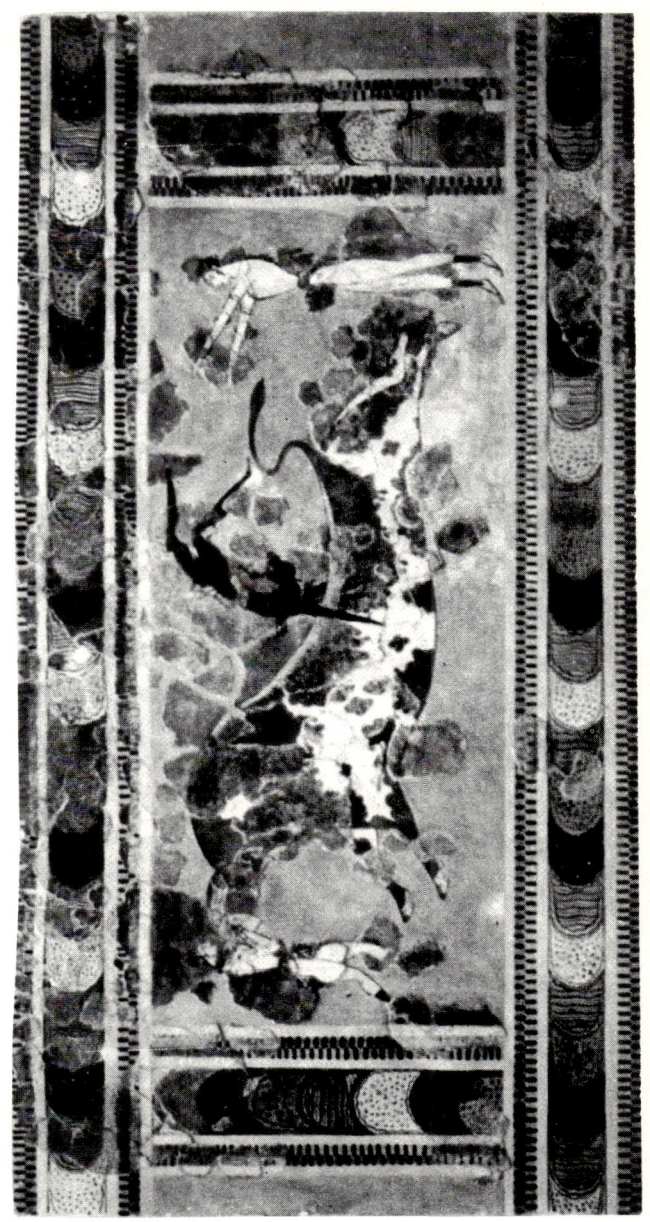

Plate III
The Toreador Fresco from Knossos. (c. 1500 B.C.) Heraclion Museum restoration, Gallery XIV.

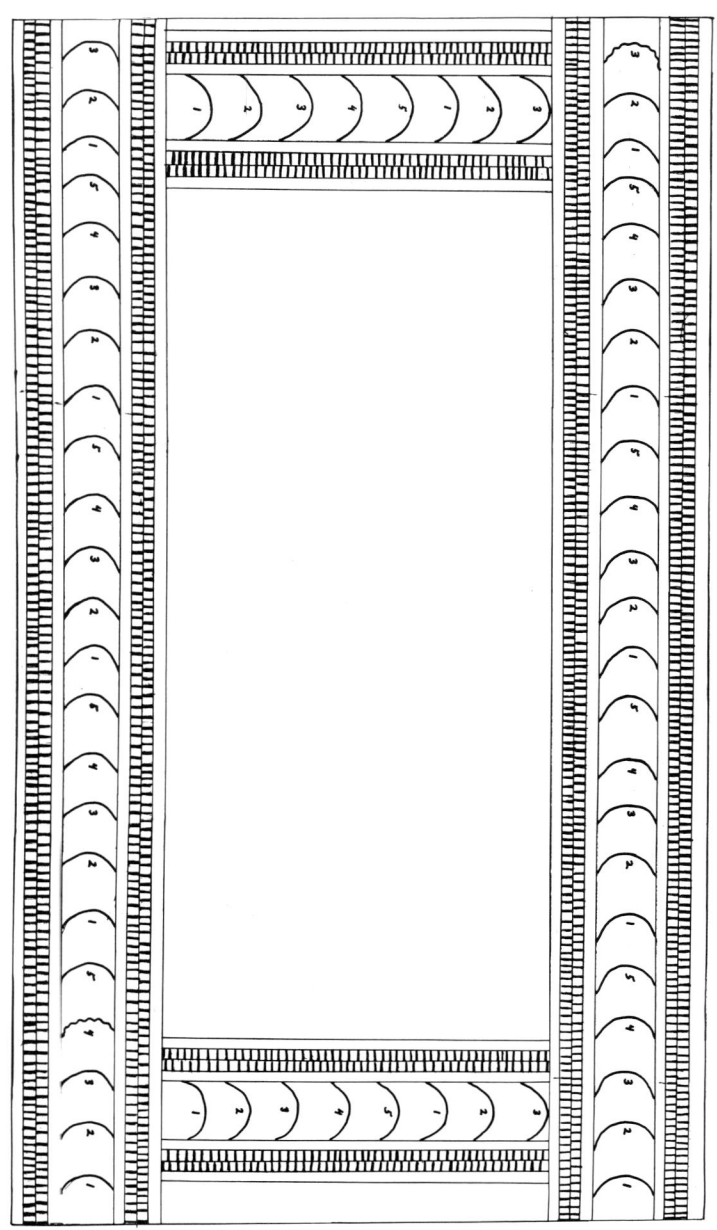

Plate IV
Diagrammatic restoration of the Toreador Fresco border.

Figure 1

Figure 2
From Shrine of the Double Axes at Knossos (c. 1400-1100 B.C.),
HM. Gallery X, Case 140.

Figure 3
From Crete (c. 2000-1500 B.C.), AM. 1938.1144. The right-hand circle is elaborated by some strokes which give the appearance of a small *bucranium*. V.E.G. Kenna, *Cretan Seals,* p. 106.

Figure 4
From Phaistos (c. 2000-1700 B.C.), HM. Gallery III, Case 40, No. 781. Design on a clay sealing. In classical times, this symbol was adopted as the badge of the Pythagoreans.

Figure 5
From Central Shrine at Knossos (c. 1700-1450 B.C.), HM. Gallery IV, Case 50.

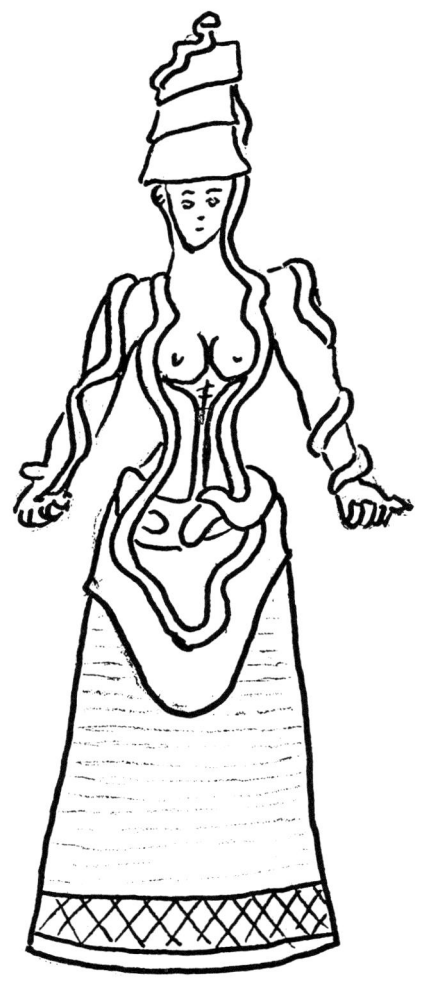

Figure 6
From Central Shrine at Knossos (c. 1700-1450 B.C.), HM. Gallery IV, Case 50.

Figure 7

Chryselephantine statuette of Minoan fertility goddess. The figure is white ivory in honor of the goddess' moon aspect. The two sacred serpents are of gold in honor of her consort, the sun god. The gold trimmed five-flounced skirt signifies the five phases of the moon. Dated Late Minoan I by J.D.S. Pendlebury. Boston Museum of Fine Arts.

Figure 8
Late Minoan engraved gem from Crete. A man-lion pursuing a man-bull. Bull-lion circle motif. AM. 1938.1069.

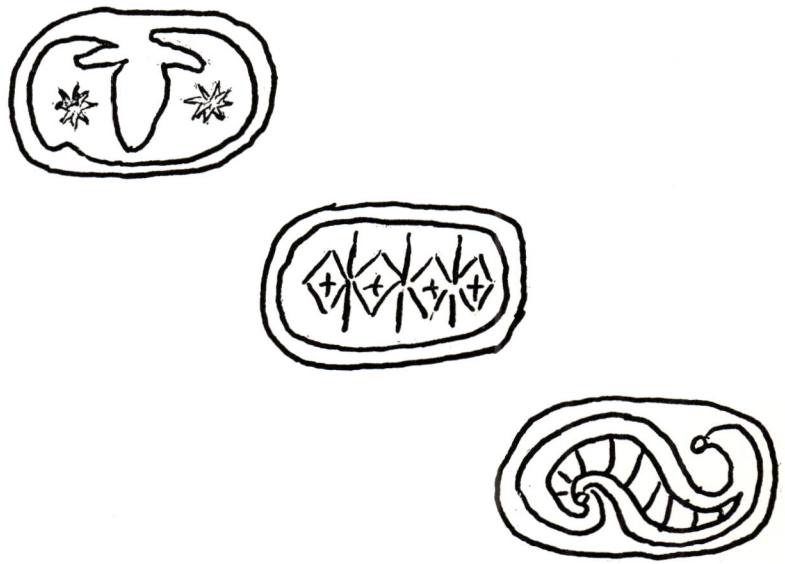

Figure 9
Middle Minoan Age prism bead. AM. AE. 1223. Left: Bucranium and two eight-rayed suns. Middle: Four lozenges signifying four or eight years. Right: S-spiral with two papyrus buds at terminals.

Figure 10
Early Minoan Age prism bead from North Crete. AM. 1910.244.
Bucranium with swastika at left and bird at right. Above a fertility
bough with eight ends.

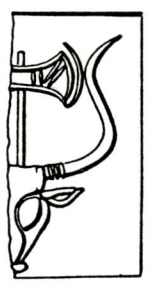

Figure 11
Late Minoan Age cylinder seal from Knossos. HM. 337. Bull's head with double axe between horns.

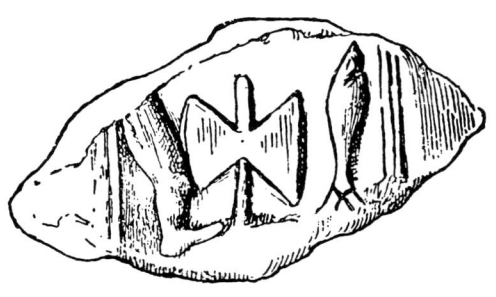

Figure 12
Early Middle Minoan Age clay sealing from Knossos. HM. 159.
Stylized double axe between glyphs of leg and fish.

But if seasonal lengths are to be kept constant, this 3 day period will be accommodated on the calendar either on a vertical track or a horizontal track depending upon the year in question. In relation to the calendar tracks, then, this 3 day period is moveable and therefore the 3 signifying marks are set apart from all tracks. On this basis, the 3 day festival would be 3 February through 5 February and would be accommodated on the calendar by the last 3 marks on the vertical track.

As we have seen, this makes sense in terms of the Cretan agricultural year. A change of weather normally occurs at the beginning of February and farmers to this day begin spring activities at that time. We may also note that in year 1 this festival will coincide with full moon and with the calendar's full moon symbol. It will, of course, not always fall at full moon, but it will approximate this in years 1, 4, and 7 of every 8 year cycle. Since 3 is one of the Goddess' numbers and the festival falls ideally at full moon, we may infer that it is a spring festival honoring the moon-goddess. However, if we look at the diagram of Figure 23, we shall see that this festival always falls on an orange track. Since orange is the sun-god's color, we should expect this festival to be related to him in some sense also.

Moving to the top horizontal track, we find the festival followed by a flight of 140 days. This would mean from 6 February to 25 June. This corresponds quite accurately with the Cretan spring as we have seen. Grain crops are harvested at the end of June and the weather begins to turn hot and dry. The end of the season also corresponds approximately with the summer solstice or longest day of the year (21 June).

Next we encounter 7 marks at the right-hand end of the top border which we omit in counting solar years. By analogy with the 3 omitted marks at the opposite end of the track, this should signify a 7 day festival, marking the beginning of the summer season. Again it is moveable on the calendar tracks and is accordingly set apart from them. To keep seasonal lengths consistent it should be counted on the outside bottom horizontal track in year 1. It begins on 26 June and extends through

2 July. In every year it falls on an orange track. This suggests that it is a festival of the sun-god and its proximity to the summer solstice bears this out. On the other hand, the number 7 is sacred to the moon-goddess and in years 1, 2, 4, 5, and 7 it falls within the seventh lunation of the lunar year. Therefore, some connection with the moon-goddess is also implied.

On the outermost bottom track we now move from right to left through a flight of 120 days. Again to keep seasonal lengths constant, we end 3 marks short of the junction with the vertical border. The 3 marks beyond the junction are omitted from a count of this year and once more signify a festival period accommodated on the calendar on different tracks in different years. This season extends from 3 July through 30 October. Hence, it corresponds very closely with the Cretan summer. The fall ploughing and sowing of grain occurs at the end of the season and the spectacular migration of the cranes southward. And according to the official meteorological records for Heraclion showing average monthly rainfall over a 30 year period, the heavy rains begin abruptly about 1 November with great consistency. The calendar indication of the end of a season marked by a festival is, then, very closely in accord with climatic conditions in Crete, which can not have changed materially in the past 3,000 years. The end of the season also coincides approximately with the autumnal setting of the Pleiades or Seven Sisters, which, as we have seen, in Hesiod's time was 26 October.

The 3 day festival would extend from 31 October through 2 November. This festival, like the preceding ones, always falls on an orange track, suggesting the sun-god, while the 3 days and the 7 Pleiades suggest the moon-goddess.

Crossing to the appropriate track for year 1 at the top of the right vertical border, we may count down 44 days, omitting the last 5 marks in the track. This is an overlap area in moon symbols and I take it to signify a 5 day festival preceding the new year and marking the end of the old year. This would mean that the 44 days would extend from 3 November through 15 December and the 5 day festival would extend from 16 December through 20 December. The last 5 marks would be counted as the last 5 festival days of the year and then we could commence a new year on 21 December at a point 5 marks up on the track for year 2. We would thus use this moon symbol once, but not twice.

The festival ends at winter solstice. This is when the old sun dies, mythically speaking, and the new sun is born. In year 1 the festival falls on a blue track. In year 2 it again falls on a blue track, but in years 3 and 4 it falls on orange tracks. All of the other festivals of the year always fall on orange tracks. This alternation every two years is paralleled by the reversal of color order every two years in the sequence pattern and by the alternation every two years of the position of the 7 and 3 day festivals on the tracks. This parallel alternation in biennial periods is too consistent a pattern to be a meaningless coincidence. It suggests a two year cycle in the alternating dance of the sun-god and moon-goddess. It is half of their 4 year cycle which in turn is half of their full 8 year cycle. The 5 days of the festival relate to the 5 phases of the moon and, hence, this festival like the other festivals of the year connects the moon-goddess and the sun-god symbolically.

The period from 3 November of year 1 through 5 February of year 2 should be considered a single season despite the fact that it straddles two solar years. Including the 5 day festival which bisects it and the 3 day festival at its end, it only totals 95 days or a little over three months. It coincides neatly with the autumn-winter rainy season in Crete as we have seen, a season which is consistently a single unit in terms of weather and agricultural activity.

If we follow the calendar through a 4 year cycle, we find that festival and seasonal dates remain exactly the same in years 1 and 2. In years 3 and 4 there is a very slight variation because the 95 days of the autumn-winter season, which straddles the new year, may only be divided into halves conveniently by alternating the lengths of the half-seasons thus produced. The result is that while seasonal lengths remain constant, the dates of festivals and seasons, except at the new year, are moved forward by one day. This is hardly a significant difference in the timing of festivals and seasons.

A table of the calendar regulation of festivals and seasons over the 4 year cycle is provided in Figure 24. There it will be seen that the spring season is always 140 days and the summer season always 120 days. This excludes the three days of the spring festival and the 7 days of the summer festival or 10 days. The autumn-winter season, which includes the 5 day solstice festival and the fall festival of 3 days, is 95 days except in leap years when it is 96 days. The total count, then, is 140 + 120 + 95 + 10 or 365 days.

It is plain, then, that the calendar does, in fact, correlate with the seasonal pattern of Crete and the agricultural year. This, of course, is in addition to its correlation with the astronomical facts of the solar-lunar cycle. This explains, I believe, why the fetsivals fall where they do. The spring and fall festivals (3 Feb. - 5 Feb. and 31 Oct. - 2 Nov.) are obviously determined by seasonal changes in the agricultural year and in a religious sense by the fertility cult implication of the autumnal death and vernal rebirth of vegetation. They do not come close at all to the equinoxes. Their origin probably goes back to the earliest stages in the evolution of Minoan religion when a simple observation of seasonal change determined the year. It was probably a bipartite year beginning in the autumn, as in Mesopotamia, and with its opposite terminal in the spring.

It is also interesting, and possibly significant, that the period from the end of the spring festival to the end of the fall festival is exactly 270 days or nine months which is the normal human gestation period. Children conceived at the spring festival would be born at about the time of the fall festival. This may be significant, since as R. F. Willetts points out, there is evidence that collective marriage was part of an initiation ritual held during a Minoan festival.[5] The Minoan goddess, Eleuthia, to be discussed in detail later, was goddess of child-birth and her special festival probably occurred in the fall since she was a Minoan predecessor of the classical Demeter whose Eleusinian festival came in the fall. It is possible, then, that the spring and fall fertility festivals were spaced this way with marriage and child-birth also in mind.

The 5 day new year festival, falling at the winter solstice, is determined by more sophisticated astronomical observation and was probably a much later development. Knowledge of the solar-lunar cycle was a step forward. This development appears to have called for a synthesis with the older seasonal system of reckoning time and the calendar looks like a response to that need. The result was that the spring and fall festivals retained a seasonal orientation while the new year festival was oriented to the winter solstice.

The 7 day summer festival, on the other hand, was oriented to both the change in season and the summer solstice. The spring season ends on either 25 June or 26 June. This is about the time of grain harvest and the beginning of hot weather. It is also the fourth or fifth day after the summer solstice. That the yearly festival should fall after the summer solstice rather than precisely on it is a consequence of its timing being governed by the moon as it will be shown. Although this was a yearly festival, there is strong evidence that it served a very special purpose at the end of every great year or 8 year cycle.

At the end of a great year the Minoan priest-king's term would have expired. For the sake of the fertility of crops, herds, and people and of the vitality and spiritual well-being of the entire state, he must either be replaced at this time or undergo a ritual death and rebirth. In short, he must either be spiritually reborn after reunion with the Goddess—the source of his divine powers—or be literally replaced by another younger king divinely sanctioned.

It is a curious fact that all known representations of the priest-king in Minoan art show him to be a beardless young man with the build of an athlete in his twenties. For instance, there is the relief fresco of a crowned young man found at Knossos which Evans suggested was quite possibly a representation of the priest-king. (Fig. 25) He is dressed in the simple loin-cloth and narrow girdle of a bull-vaulter. He wears a crown decorated with five lilies and three peacock plumes. As we have seen, the lily is a flower sacred to the goddess and five is her mystic number as moon-goddess. The three plumes would also be in her honor. But the total of five plus three would, of course, be eight which is the sun-god's number and the number of years in the calendar cycle. There are also two spiral ornaments in the crown spiralling in opposite directions which suggest the way in which the calendar is read. He wears an interesting necklace which Evans says is made up of ornaments shaped like the lilies in his crown.[6] Unfortunately a fragment of the fresco is missing at the neck and shoulder of the figure so that we can not be certain how many lily ornaments existed in the original, but judging from those remaining, it was probably a total of eight. If so, this is again the sun-god's number which would be an appropriate badge for the priest-king as his temporal incarnation. This and other figures thought to represent the priest-king show him as a young man.

Could the priest-kings of Knossos have been ritually invested with divine power at say, the age of 18 and at the end of a great year ritually sacrificed to the goddess at, say, 27 years of age? Possibly. But it is more probable that they were (at least in the late period from which the Toreador fresco dates) reinvested with refreshed divine power at the end of a great year after a ceremony and a surrogate sacrifice.

But when would such a ceremony be held? It might have been held at the winter solstice festival terminating the eighth year of the calendar cycle. But I believe there is a more likely alternative. According to Robert Graves' interpretation in his *Greek Myths,* sacred kings reigned for a period of 100 lunations after which followed an additional period terminated by their death or by a ceremony of symbolic death and rebirth.[7] This additional period dated from the end of the great year and fell at the seventh full moon after the shortest day. Graves also offers an interesting interpretation of the myth of the halcyon or kingfisher which helps to solve this problem.[8] According to Graves, the "halcyon days" were seven days before and seven days after the solstice, peaceful days when the sea was smooth and the hen-halcyon built a floating nest and hatched her young.[9]

The traditional story also adds that at this time she carried her dead mate on her back over the sea mourning for him. Graves interprets the fourteen days as a moon-number, it being the number of days between new moon and full moon. The halcyon is one of the bird epiphanies of the moon-goddess, and Graves sees the myth as a poetic image of the death of the sacred king, spouse of the moon-goddess, and of his rebirth at the end of a great year falling at the solstice and preceded and followed by the seven halcyon days.

Now all this ties in with the calendar in a most interesting way. The solar-lunar cycle of the calendar is eight years and this amounts to 99 lunations. Graves' reference to sacred kings reigning 100 lunations may be seen to be a round figure, 99 lunations being more exact. The mythic evidence pointing to the death of sacred kings at the seventh full moon following the shortest day (winter solstice and new moon coincide on this day in this year) would fall exactly on the last day of the seven day summer festival. And if, as the halcyon myth suggests, there are fourteen special days rather than merely seven to be celebrated at this time, to mark a great year, it seems likely that they would be the seven days of the usual annual festival plus the seven days preceding them at the end of the season. If this is so, then the summer solstice would fall on the third day of the fourteen day festival exactly eleven days before full moon. And the entire fourteen day festival would appear to have a rather neat symmetry. There would be two opening days, as it were, to the festival, then summer solstice day. Then four days to the end of the season. Then seven days to full moon on the last day of the festival. In this year, and only in this year of the 8 year cycle, full moon falls precisely on the full moon symbol of the calendar. The timing of the seven day annual festival four days after the summer solstice is necessary to coordinate this more significant fourteen day festival with the solstice and a full moon at the end of the festival. And the unique correlation of a full moon at this time of the year with a full moon symbol on the calendar bears this out.

I should like to add that there are good reasons for connecting the halcyon myth with the Minoan moon-goddess. First because, as many Minoan art objects attest, the goddess most frequently appears to man in the form of a bird. This is her usual epiphany, and Aphrodite's dove and Athena's owl are later classical survivals of this tradition. We are also told that the halcyon bears her dead mate away on her back, mourning for him. There are several Cretan seals engraved with the motif of a goddess bearing on her back a dead animal, usually a bull. One, dated Late Minoan and, hence, contemporary with the calendar, is in the Ashmolean and is a Cretan seal (A.M. 1941. 120). (Fig. 26) The bull on this seal could very well represent the surrogate victim killed at the end of a great year in place of the sacred king who, of course, is associated with the solar bull. His spouse, the moon-goddess, mourns his death and bears him away, like the kingfisher does her mate, over her shoulder on her back.

The conclusion I draw from this accumulation of evidence is that the Minoan king underwent a ceremonial death and rebirth at a fourteen day festival which occurred not at the end of the eight year cycle, but half a year later at summer solstice and full moon. In other words, this ceremony took place not in the eighth but in the ninth year of a king's term. This may explain the confusion about the length of the reign of Minos caused by varying references from ancient sources some of which speak of Minos as an eight year king while others say nine. Homer, as we have seen, calls him a nine-year king. There is, of course, a sense in which both traditions are right. His reign is governed by an eight year solar-lunar cycle, but his ritual renewal falls in the following ninth year.

We have seen that the moon symbols on the calendar are arranged as they are to indicate, among other things, periodic moments when solar and lunar events of importance coincide or when lunar events of importance coincide with calendar festivals. Since the moon symbols are fixed, they can correspond symbolically with actual lunar phases only a limited number of times in an 8 year cycle. We have observed that the winter solstice falls every year precisely on the mark opposite the convex tip of the new moon symbol. But where do the other solar events of importance fall in relation to the calendar symbols?

The spring equinox always falls on the second new moon symbol from the left on the top border. The four day marks where it falls in the four tracks of the four year cycle bracket the first four days of this new moon symbol. It appears, then, that the spring equinox is associated symbolically with the new moon. This is also true of the fall equinox which always falls on the second new moon symbol from the left on the bottom border and brackets the first three days of that symbol.

On the other hand, the summer solstice always falls on the last blue, full moon symbol on the right of the top border. The four day marks of the four tracks bracket the complete symbol or seven days. Hence, it appears that the summer solstice is associated with the full moon, whereas both equinoxes and the winter solstice are associated with the new moon.

If the placement of moon symbols along the borders has symbolic meaning beyond what we have already discovered, we should expect to find a periodic correlation between the actual occurrence of the new or full moon, the equinoxes and solstices, and the associated proper symbols. And so we do. There are four and only four such correlations in an eight year cycle.[10] We have already seen one of these correlations. Every eight years a new moon occurs on the winter solstice and correlates with the day mark opposite the top of the new moon symbol at the bottom of the left-hand vertical border. This correlation is, of course, the basis for the entire calendar system. Consequently a new moon can not fall precisely on any of the other three stations of the year. But new moon or full moon, as appropriate to the particular station, may fall somewhere on the new moon or full moon symbol associated with the three stations. In other words, it may fall on the appropriate symbol as bracketed by the day marks discussed above.

Such correlations occur at the equinoxes in years 1 and 3, the moon's numbers, and at the solstices in years 4 and 8, the sun's numbers. The end of lunation 3 in year 1 gives us a new moon 2 days before the spring equinox and on the calendar new moon symbol. This is the only time this occurs in an eight year cycle. The end of lunation 34 in year 3 gives us a new moon 1 day before the fall equinox and on the new moon symbol. This, too, is unique in every eight year cycle. Lunation 44 in year 4 gives us a full moon 6 days after the summer solstice and on the full moon symbol, which is again unique. As we have seen above the summer solstice is associated with the full moon rather than the new moon. And, finally, lunation 99 at the end of year 8 gives us a new moon on the new moon symbol which is the starting point for another eight year cycle. So there are exactly four such correlations with the four stations of the year in an eight year cycle.

There are seven additional correlations with the festivals of the year. The spring and fall festivals always fall on a full moon symbol. The winter festival always falls on a new moon symbol. And the seven day summer festival shares a part of two symbols, which function as full moon and new moon symbols at this point in their sequence.

Lunation 2 in year 1 gives us a full moon on the first day of the spring festival and consequently on the full moon symbol. Lunation 36 in year 3 gives us a full moon on the last day of the fall festival and therefore on the proper symbol. Lunation 37 at the end of year 3 gives us a new moon on the first day of the winter festival and accordingly on the correct symbol. This is the year in which a thirteenth month is intercalated. The second intercalation at the end of year 6, which is lunation 74, gives us a new moon 1 day before the new moon symbol and 2 days before the festival. The correlation is, therefore, imperfect but approximate. Lunation 99 at the end of year 8 has already been mentioned. Since it correlates with the winter solstice, it naturally correlates with the winter festival as well.

The remaining three correlations are with the summer festival. Lunation 56 in year 5 gives us a new moon on the fourth day of the summer festival and on the new moon symbol. Lunation 7 in year 1 gives us a full moon on the last day of the summer festival, and it falls on the full moon symbol in that year. This correlation is the important one discussed already in connection with the ritual death of the priest-king at the end of his term. For lunation 7 of year 1 is equivalent to lunation 106 of year 9 if we carry the count of lunations beyond an eight year cycle. It is the seventh lunation after a full eight year cycle and, as we have seen, evidence points to this as the occasion of the halcyon days, the fourteen days of festival celebrated at the end of a king's term.

We have in all, then, eleven correlations of the moon symbols on the calendar with periodic solar and lunar events and with festivals of the year. Since these particular solar and lunar events can only occur once each in an eight year period at precise points in the cycle, it is certainly significant that the appropriate calendar symbols correlate with them. The seasons of the sun and the festivals of the moon are clearly indicated in this amazing ritual calendar.

NOTES

[1] Hutchinson, *Prehistoric Crete,* p. 38.
[2] Frazer, *The New Golden Bough,* p. 361.
[3] Based on official meteorological observations for Heraclion over a 30 year period. J. M. Christoforakis, *Crete* (Athens, 1961), p. 20.
[4] Hutchinson, *Prehistoric Crete,* p. 38.
[5] Willetts, *Cretan Cults and Festivals,* p. 117.
[6] William A. McDonald, *Progress Into the Past* (Bloomington, Indiana, 1969), p. 136; a quotation from Evans, *The Palace of Minos.*
[7] Robert Graves, *Greek Myths* (New York, 1959), p. 16 and p. 18.
[8] Graves, *White Goddess,* pp. 193-194.
[9] Graves has in mind the winter solstice. However, he mentions that Pliny writes that the halcyon is rarely to be seen except on the winter solstice, the summer solstice, or at the setting of the Pleiades (Graves, *White Goddess,* p. 194). Apparently the associations of the myth are not strictly limited to the winter solstice.
[10] Solstices and equinoxes are calculated here to the nearest full day in a hypothetical year when the winter solstice falls on 21 December.

Chapter VI

BULL, LION, SERPENT AND GRIFFON

Iamblichus remarks in his life of Pythagoras: "Orpheus said that the eternal essence of number is the most providential principle of the universe, of heaven, of earth, and of the nature intermediate to these; and, more, that it is the basis of the permanency of divine natures, gods, and demons."[1] Since there is reason to believe that Orphic number theory had its origin in Minoan Crete, it should prove interesting to explore the mathematics of the calendar to see if there are any patterns of symmetry with possible implications.

It is plain that the calendar was designed for the proper timing of religious rituals and festivals of the moon-goddess. Of course, it no doubt had practical uses as well in the predicting of tides and in governing the agricultural and pastoral activities of the year, but even these concerns would be viewed in a religious context. Its mathematical aspect would probably be seen as a manifestation of divine order in the universe. Accordingly the occurrence of certain numbers and their factors or multiples would be likely to be construed as mystically significant. The importance of symbolic numbers sacred to the moon-goddess or the sun-god has already been amply demonstrated. But perhaps there are more subtle numerical correspondences inherent in the structure of the calendar which we have not yet explored.

The ancient Sumerian year as well as the Egyptian year was 360 days increased to 365 by a festival that was not considered a part of the year proper. In Egypt the god Thoth was said to have won at draughts with the moon-goddess the seventy-second part of all of the days of the year which he compounded into five whole days and added to the 360 day Egyptian year to make 365 days in all.[2] As we have seen, the calendar appears to have indicated by an overlapping moon symbol a five day festival at the end of every year which implies that in Crete also at this period the official year was considered to be 360 days—the extra five days being in some sense outside it.

As the ancient Sumerians knew, the number 360 has many beauties. It is 6 x 60 and 60 is exactly divisible by 2, 3, 4, 5, 6, 10, 12, 15, 20, and 30. Furthermore, 360 is the number of degrees into which they divided a circle and we use that division to this day. Indeed, they worked out a sexagesimal system of counting or a system which combines the decimal system with a system based on the number 60.[3] The 360 day year, for the Sumerians at least, was a way of bringing the counting of time into correspondence with the counting of degrees in a circle, the twelve houses of the Zodiac, and their sexagesimal system.

The Minoans are not credited with knowledge of the sexagesimal system.[4] The clay tablets of Linear A and Linear B script upon which they kept accounts for inventory purposes give evidence of a system of numerical notation based upon 10.

Nevertheless, the number 60 appears to have had special significance to them. James Walter Graham made extensive measurements of the architectural layout of the palaces at Mallia, Gournia, Phaistos, and Knossos, which yielded some interesting results. The evidence he collected indicated that the Minoans used a standard foot-length equal to approximately 11 15/16 in. or 30.36 cm. as a unit of measurement. Major architectural elements of the palaces appear to have been layed out in round numbers of such Minoan feet. Graham discovered that an interval of 60 Minoan feet occurred so frequently as to be noteworthy and he suggests that it is possible that the Minoans used a sexagesimal system for some purposes as well as counting by tens for other purposes.[5] Graham does not suggest that the number 60 was used for its symbolic significance, but I am inclined to think that this is the likely explanation.

The calendar shows that their 360 day year provided an opportunity for thinking mathematically in factors of 60 and they appear to have done so in dividing the year. As we have seen, their lunar year was divided into 12 months and 60 moon phases.

But more surprising is their division of the seasons on a basis of twelfths of a 360 day year. The spring season together with the ten adjoining days of the spring and summer festivals is 150 days or 5/12 of 360 days. The summer season of 120 days is 4/12 of 360 days. And the fall-winter season, including the three day fall festival, but excluding the five days before winter solstice, which are not part of the official year, is 90 days or 3/12 of 360 days. Thus the 360 day year is divided neatly into twelfths (3/12, 4/12, 5/12) of ascending magnitude. This, of course, corresponds with the division of the lunar year into twelve months. The number twelve occurs so frequently in the calendar that one is led to suspect that it served a symbolic purpose as well as a mathematical one.

Another number which occurs too frequently in the calendar to be ignored is eleven. There are eleven days more in the solar year than the lunar year and the calendar is designed to accommodate this fact. The number of days in the fall-winter season, excluding festivals, is 95 - 7 or 88 days. Here we have the significant solar number 8 multiplied by 11. And the number of moon symbols that are actually traversed in counting days on the top and bottom borders is 44 or 22 on each border—again a multiple of 11. What is more, the number of lunations in an entire eight year solar-lunar cycle is exactly 99 or 9 x 11.

There also appears to be a significant alternation between 11 and 12. For if we count all the moon symbols on the horizontal borders, we get 23 + 23 or 46. And if we subtract the 22 symbols we actually use on either border, we get 46 - 22 or 24 which is twice 12. A similar alternation between 7 and 8 occurs on the vertical borders. There are 8 moon symbols on each vertical border. But in counting days on alternate years we traverse 7 symbols on one border and 8 symbols on the other and then reverse the process. The result is an alternation of 7 and 8.

We are already familiar with 7 as one of the goddess' numbers and with 8 as one of the sun-god's numbers. Hence, the alternation of these two numbers would seem to imply symbolically the parting and joining of the sun and moon in the labyrinthine dance of the calendar. But suppose we combine the 22 moon symbols traversed on a horizontal border with the 7 symbols traversed on a vertical border. The result is a significant surprise, for 22 is the measure of the circumference of a circle when the diameter is 7. It is the well-known mathematical proportion called *pi,* which is approximated by the ratio 22/7. Expressed decimally it is 2.1416 etc. The ratio, of course, can never be absolutely determined since it involves one in an infinite regress. Knowing the Minoan propensity for number mysticism, I am unwilling to dismiss this as an accidental coincidence. For symbolically it implies that the labyrinth of the calendar is an infinite circle demonstrating the eternal return which is the ultimate principle of the Great Goddess herself.

But what is the significance of the alternation of 11 and 12? According to myth there were exactly twelve Titans. The Titans were giants who ruled before the Olympian Gods of Greece defeated them in battle under the leadership of Zeus. The canonical number twelve was preserved in Greek religion. Only twelve gods held Mount Olympus and records from classical times show that sacrifices were sometimes made specifically in the name of "The Twelve Gods."[6] The twelve Titans of Greek myth represent twelve figures of importance in the earlier religion of the Pelasgians and Minoans and probably other Aegean peoples who were established in the lands that the early Greeks invaded. The defeat of the Titans by the Olympians is simply a mythic way of expressing the victory of the Olympian religion over the older native cults.

According to Herodotus the Pelasgians did not originally worship a plurality of gods and, as we have seen, this is also true of the early Minoans.[7] They worshipped a goddess and her semi-divine son, the king. The twelve Titans were, therefore, not literally gods in the Greek sense.

But what were they then? Hesiod helps us here. Hesiod says that the word "Titan" means "to stretch" and he adds that they were so called because they stretched out their hands of ten fingers.[8] This stretching out of ten fingers is precisely the gesture of a great many statuettes of the goddess from various sites dating from the period c. 1400-1100 B.C. A good example from the Shrine of the Double Axes at Knosssos may be seen in Figure 2. As I have suggested in Chapter II, these figurines of the goddess stretching out ten fingers in a symbolic gesture is a reference to the famous Dactyls or fingers. And as we have seen, the Dactyls were associated with a sacred cult of the Minoan goddess. According to one tradition they were created by the goddess as attendants upon her divine lover. And another tradition refers to Herakles as their leader and tells us that Herakles brought them from Crete to Olympia to found the Olympic Games, a religious calendric festival.

The Herakles tradition referred to above mentions only five male Dactyls who were competitors in ritual games. But as R. F. Willetts has shown, there is good reason to believe there were more than five and that they were not all male. He connects them with the Kouretes and Korybantes and sees in them a tribal ritual involving youths and maidens in initiation rites, which feature athletic contests and dances as part of a ceremony of sacred marriage.[9] The canonical number of Dactyls, then, was certainly ten—five male and five female.

They were celebrants of a ritual of sacred marriage which all young men and young women of the community who had attained the proper age might be represented by in a public calendar festival. The ten young people chosen to represent the Dactyls in any year would partake of divinity as communicants and all of the initiates would do so also vicariously. Ultimately, the divine principle celebrated was the sacred marriage of the priest-king as sun-god and the moon-goddess. But since the solar year is divided by the two solstices, the mimetic ritual called for two twin kings of the year to represent the waxing and the waning sun. These participants in the ritual were the principals and they raised the total number from ten to twelve.

To recapitulate, then, the twelve Titans of Greek tradition derive from the ten Dactyls plus their leaders, the two twin kings of the year. The significance of the alternation of eleven and twelve in the calendar is the alternation in the reign of these solar twins.

As we have seen in Chapter II, these twin kings are frequently represented in the motif that I have called the bull-lion circle. And there is reason to believe that the bull dies at the summer solstice festival. Artistic representations of the motif frequently show the lion attacking the bull and never show the bull goring the lion. Symbolically interpreted this means that the bull is the waxing sun of the spring season who is destroyed by the lion, the waning sun of the summer season. This interpretation is strengthened by the fact that the Zodiacal constellation of Taurus, the bull, was a spring sign in the late second millennium B.C. (the period of the calendar) while the constellation of Leo, the lion, was a summer sign. The Minoans are known to have had many cultural contacts with the ancient Middle East so it is likely that they were aware of this astrological lore stemming from Mesopotamia.

The longer of the two seasons is the spring season of the bull. Therefore, the greater number, 12, would appear to be the number of the bull season while 11 would be the number of the shorter lion season. Furthermore, the bull, representing the waxing sun, is clearly the principal calendar beast in Minoan iconography, and as principal in a ritual involving twelve participants he would logically be the twelfth. Although he is the principal, he is so in the sense that a tragic hero or protagonist is principal in the ritual of Greek drama and he is destroyed in this ritual by his antagonist, the lion, whose number 11, a feminine number, relates him to the goddess in her death aspect.

The alternation of 11 and 12 as calendar numbers may now be seen as symbolic of the cyclical alternation of the seasons represented by the two calendar beasts of the year, the bull and the lion. The alternation of 7 and 8 represents the rhythm of the moon and the sun. And the combination of one member from each of these pairs, 22 (2 x 11) and 7, represents the eternal circle of the labyrinth of the calendar, which like a universal symbol reconciles all opposites in infinity.

Pentheus in the *Bacchae* of Euripides charges the god, Dionysus, to appear "as a wild bull, as a many-headed snake, or as a fire-breathing lion."[10] We may recognize here two of the calendar beasts of the year, the bull and the lion. Dionysus is a god of Pre-Olympian origin and the myths about him tell us that he was a type of the sun-god who dies and is reborn and undergoes transformations in form. As we have seen, the spring is the season of the sun-god as bull and the summer is his season as lion, for as the circle in which they move implies, the two are ultimately one, having only changed in form. But, as the calendar shows, there are three seasons to the Minoan year and the bull and lion account for only two. What form does the ever-changing sun-god take in the fall-winter season?

Euripides gives the answer, the serpent. We might have expected this from the serpentine course the sun-god dances in his biennial alternations with the moon-goddess. That the identification of the serpent with the fall-winter season is correct, may be seen on a seal from Knossos dated Middle Minoan III (H.M. 1597). The seal has four engraved faces, a sun number. (Fig. 27) The first face shows a simple labyrinth motif—the crossed rectangle. The second face features two standing birds which appear to be cranes. The third face shows a large serpent with four cranes flying in V-formation above him. This recalls the autumnal migration of the cranes cited by Hesiod as the traditional sign of fall, and as we have seen, their migration coincides with the setting of the Pleiades and the fall festival of the calendar. The fourth face presents six paired, parallel labyrinth motifs which probably have the calendric significance of six or possibly twelve years. On one seal, then, we find the cranes and their migration, traditionally a sign of fall, associated with a calendric motif and with a serpent specifically shown with the cranes flying above him. The fall-winter is, then, the season of the sun-god as serpent.

It is not difficult to see the poetic rightness of the sun-god as serpent in this season. It is in the middle of this season that the sun dies and is reborn at winter solstice. Who has not noticed that snakes periodically shed their old skins and come forth anew as if reborn. And what living creature is anatomically more appropriate than a serpent in symbolizing eternal return. Can any other animal coil in a spiral or comfortably assume the shape of a circle with tail in mouth? In addition, the phallic shape of the serpent suggests the fertilizing potency of the sun, which the Egyptians recognized by adorning their Pharaoh's crown with a golden serpent's head. The Minoans, like the Egyptians, had not been conditioned to see in the snake a symbol of evil. This reaction is a product of Hebrew and Christian tradition wherein the serpent is cast in the role of the devil. The Minoan sun-serpent was a benevolent one—a guardian of the household and a healer of the sick—as its appearance on the Caduceus of Hermes—and the modern medical profession—attests.

We have, then, a beast for all seasons—the bull of spring, the lion of summer and the serpent of the season of rains. Yet there remains one more. The official year was tuned to the magical number of 360 days. The five remaining days of the winter solstice festival was symbolized by a fourth calendar beast, the Griffon.

The Griffon is a composite creature with the head and wings of an eagle, the paws and frame of a lion, and the tail of a serpent. The Griffon is feminine for she represents the goddess as well as the lion and serpent, who in an ultimate sense are only emanations from her all-inclusive substance. Her composite nature reflects this universality. As we have seen, the goddess usually manifests herself to mortal men as a bird, and the bird forms in which she appears are several, although restricted to a sacred few. The crane, the partridge, the dove, the kingfisher, and the wild goose or swan appear, from the evidence of art, to be her most frequent epiphanies. But as eagle-griffon, she is a bird of prey. This is appropriate because she is the taker of life as well as the giver of life and nothing can live but what it lives on another form of the life substance. Life feeds upon itself and the Griffon represents that constant flux of temporal forms. Therefore, the Griffon is emblematic of the beginning and the end of all things. No wonder she presides over the end of the year, which is also the beginning of the year, the five days before winter solstice.

But if the Griffon is a symbol tying all things together, why is the bull absent from the composition? In a sense, he is not absent since the Griffon slays the bull with her lion's claws. This calendric unity may be seen in an interesting seal from Zakros dated Late Minoan I or II (H.M. Gallery IX, case 124, unnumbered seal). The seal displays a composite design with a bull's skull in the center, eagles' wings spreading laterally, and lion's paws below. (Fig. 28) Above the bull's skull is a loop which I take to be the top portion of a sacral knot, tying all of the other elements of the composition together. Such sacral knots are a well-known motif in Minoan art and were believed by Evans to have religious significance. If so, the key to the significance of the sacral knots may be inferred from this design. In most instances, the sacral knot is worn by the goddess or her priestesses. A good example is the famous fresco fragment from Knossos known popularly as "La Parisienne." (Fig. 29) We have seen from much other evidence that the essence of the Goddess is a unifying principle—a principle which ties all things together. Her sacral knot, then, would be a most appropriate symbol for this particular function. And it appears to function that way in the Zakros seal cited above.

The design on the seal is not literally a Griffon, but its symbolic function is the same, tying together calendar beasts—a Griffon's wings, a lion's paws, and a bull's skull. The bull, who is missing in the Griffon proper, here appears. The fact that the bull is represented by a fleshless skull suggests the yearly death of the solar bull and probably also the sacrifice of a bull at the appropriate festival.

The Griffon is a very frequent motif in Minoan art, and its sacred character as a symbol is well attested by the kind of context in which it is often found. Most notable is the wingless Griffon fresco which was found in the ceremonial throne room in the Palace at Knossos.[11] I am not referring to the attractive but fanciful restoration which now may be seen on each side of the throne in the Palace as restored today. What remains of the original fresco from this site (it was badly damaged by fire), I have seen in the Heraclion Museum. It is a large wingless Griffon, seated, with tail and beak upraised amid foliage—probably lilies. Its original proximity to the ceremonial throne bears witness to its importance as a ritual symbol. The gypsum throne has a sun-disc between its forward legs and the back has a scalloped edge featuring four arcs on each side for a total of eight in honor of the priest-king and a single ninth arc in the central position at the top in honor of the goddess.

The throne room also has a large sunken basin, which the throne faces, and which may be entered in a spiral fashion clockwise by descending six steps and turning right.[12] It was probably used by the priest-king in a ritual of death and rebirth symbolically acted by spiralling into a bath of sanctified water in a clockwise fashion, signifying death, and then spiralling out again, in a counter-clockwise fashion, signifying rebirth from the bath of the womb.[13] The six steps suggest that the ritual occurred at the winter solstice festival when five days mark the dying year while the sixth day would be the day of the solstice itself, 21 December, when the new year is born. The discovery of the Griffon fresco in this location is therefore not surprising since the Griffon is the calendar beast of these particular five holy days.

Now that we have identified the four calendar beasts of the year—the bull, the lion, the serpent, and the Griffon—with their proper seasons, the next step will be an attempt to place the fresco calendar in a more precise chronological frame.

NOTES

[1] Graves, *White Goddess*, p. 269; quotation from Iamblichus.
[2] Frazer, *The New Golden Bough*, p. 323.
[3] Rene Taton, *History of Science, Ancient and Medieval Science* (New York, 1963), p. 90.
[4] Hutchinson, *Prehistoric Crete*, p. 89.
[5] Graham, *The Palaces of Crete*, p. 226.
[6] Willetts, *Cretan Cults and Festivals*, p. 291.
[7] Graves, *White Goddess*, p. 418; quotation from Herodotus.
[8] Graves, *White Goddess*, p. 415; quotation from Hesiod.
[9] Willetts, *Cretan Cults and Festivals*, p. 117.
[10] Graves, *White Goddess*, p. 134.
[11] In the Heraclion Museum, Gallery XIV. Discussed in *Guide to the Archaeological Museum of Heraclion* (Athens, 1968) Stylianou Alexiou, p. 99. Also discussed in Pendlebury, *The Archaeology of Crete*, p. 200.
[12] There are two other so-called "lustral baths" of this type in the Palace, one in the northwest corner and another in the southwest corner. These also are built to be entered in a spiral fashion by descending steps and turning. In addition to those in the Palace proper, there are four more such in outlying buildings at Knossos: in the Little Palace, the Royal Villa, the South House, and the South-East House. These are thought by R. W. Hutchinson to have had a ceremonial use. Hutchinson, *Prehistoric Crete*, p. 175.
[13] There is evidence that when sacred kings were actually killed, sometimes by designing usurpers, they were killed in a lustral bath of this kind. There is a legend that Minos, probably a Mycenaean Greek Minos, was killed in a bath in Sicily by the priestess of Cocalus while he was there on a naval expedition. And Agamemnon, who was probably a sacred king in Mycenae, was killed in a bath at the instigation of Clytemnestra and her lover, Aegisthus. It appears that usurpers were nevertheless pious and murdered the king in a sacred bath to insure his rebirth.

CHAPTER VII

THESEUS AND ARIADNE

Up to this point I have been content to consider the Toreador Fresco a product of the Late Bronze Age at Knossos without attempting to establish its date more precisely. Minoan religion, in which the calendar had its roots, unquestionably developed throughout a long evolution and the calendar reflects a late stage in that process. The step to be taken next is to place it—in so far as that is possible—in its proper prehistorical context—not primarily in terms of absolute date, but in relation to the particular stage in Late Bronze Age religion where it appears to consistently fit.

Of course, the starting point for any such attempt is provided by the archaeological evidence as interpreted by qualified experts. Sir Arthur Evans, in the many years of his study of Minoan culture, revised his dating of the Toreador Fresco several times. Originally he assigned it to the end of Late Minoan I a.[1] Later he favored a somewhat later dating, assigning it to Late Minoan II or possibly Late Minoan I b.[2] In his earliest dating, in absolute terms, he placed it "shortly preceding 1500 B.C."[3]

Evans, however, did not know that the Linear B script which he found at Knossos on clay tablets was, in fact, a syllabary for writing an early form of the Greek language. After Michael Ventris decoded the Linear B script, it was possible to decipher many of the Knossos tablets and the Greek inventory accounts there recorded plainly indicated a Mycenaean Greek occupation of the Palace. This fact, together with other complementary evidence, led some scholars to consider a later date for the last phase of the Palace more in keeping with the dating of the apparently contemporary Mycenaean palaces using the same script on the Greek mainland.

88

Specifically, the Toreador Fresco, and the fragments of other frescoes found with it, appear to date from the last phase of the Palace on the basis of stratigraphy and associated finds. If these deductions are sound, the dating of the Toreador Fresco could logically be assumed to be considerably later than the tentative dates assigned by Evans. At present expert opinion is not in unanimity on this problem.[4]

However, for the purpose in hand what is needed is a set of limiting dates between which the fresco may be reasonably assumed to have been painted. The dates assigned by Evans provide an upward limit of c. 1500 B.C. Recently Professor Leonard R. Palmer has argued cogently that the last Palace at Knossos was destroyed in the twelfth century B.C. after the destruction of the Mycenaean palaces of the mainland.[5] His theory is that there were in all three great palaces in pre-historic Knossos. The first two were entirely "Minoan." He sees the second of these "Minoan" palaces as destroyed or partially destroyed by Mycenaean Greeks from the mainland about 1400 B.C. The third and last great Palace he believes was a "Creto-Mycenaean Palace" inhabited by a Greek Minos, grandfather of the Idomeneus of Crete who fought in the Trojan War. He assigns the Toreador Fresco to this last Palace.[6] Accordingly, if his theory is sound, the fresco could not be earlier than c. 1400 B.C. and might be as late as c. 1200 B.C.

Let us accept these dates, then, as upper and lower limiting dates, i.e., c. 1500 B.C. - c. 1200 B.C. The problem is to discover what stage of development religion at Knossos had probably reached within these limiting dates.

The Linear B tablets from Knossos provide some clues. The precise dating of the tablets is likewise controversial, but it is clear that they date within the limits set above and most probably close to the middle of these extremes.[7] Accordingly their testimony provides a logical starting point for inquiry.

The tablets served a quite utilitarian purpose. They were records of supplies of oil and wine and other commodities received or dispensed from store rooms. Among them are occasional references to offerings made to divinities. And the divinities named may be recognized with reasonable accuracy.

The feminine divinities mentioned outnumber the masculine seven to four.[8] And out of the total of eleven divinities which appear, eight may be identified as native Minoan while three appear to be imports from abroad.

Among the goddesses we find Potnia Dapu²ritojo, who has been identified as the "Lady of the Labyrinth."[9] "Potnia" is feminine and means "mistress" or more literally "the potent one." "Dapu²ritojo" is an epithet for the place of the "labrys" or the Labyrinth. We also find Hera, known to have originated in Crete, Diwia, a feminine form of Zeus, Eleuthia, a patroness of child-birth with a cult at Amnisos near Knossos, Erinu, Pipituna, and Potnia Atana.

All of these Goddesses appear to be of Minoan origin. There can be no doubt about Hera who, as we have seen, is associated with the sun-king, Herakles, who brought the Dactyls from Crete to establish the games at Olympia. Diwia, being a feminine counterpart of Zeus, reflects a connection with Cretan-born Zeus rather than with the later Olympian Zeus whose spouse was Hera. Eleuthia's sacred cave at Amnisos, the seaport for Knossos, is mentioned by Homer in the *Odyssey*. She is certainly a Cretan divinity as the evidence assembled by R. F. Willetts clearly attests.[10] Erinu appears to be related to the Erinys or Furies. They, in turn, are related to Demeter, one of whose epithets was Demeter Erinys. And the Furies as well as Demeter were probably derived from the chthonic underworld aspect of the Minoan Great Goddess.[11] Pipituna is identified by Emily Vermeule as a forerunner of Diktynna, a hunting goddess worshipped in Crete in classical times.[12] She appears to derive from the virgin huntress aspect of the Minoan Great Goddess, paralleling the classical Greek Artemis who was also so derived.

The remaining feminine divinity is Potnia Atana. She is almost certainly an early representative of the great goddess of Athens, Athena. In her Mycenaean stage of development, Athena was closer to the Minoan "snake goddess" of fertility than to her later image as warrior maiden. Myth as well as the distant background of the Erectheum on the Athenian acropolis associate her with the snake and the olive tree—both fertility symbols.[13] Her ultimate derivation appears to have been Minoan or at least Aegean and pre-Greek. But she was already at home in Athens in Mycenaean times and was probably adopted by the Greeks from the earlier Pelasgian inhabitants of Athens. For these reasons, I am inclined to see her as a distant relative of the other feminine deities at Knossos who was brought in by the Achaean overlords for whom the records on the Linear B tablets were kept.

Of the male divinities mentioned on the tablets two appear to be natives and two strangers at Knossos. As for Zeus, even in classical times he was reputed to have been born in Crete. The original Cretan Zeus, however, was very unlike the thunderbolt-hurler who reigned supreme over all the gods of Olympus. He was a type of the dying and resurrecting sun-god, spouse of the moon-goddess, and definitely subordinate to her.[14] It would appear to be this Cretan Zeus that the tablets refer to, especially since the dominance of feminine deities is reflected by their outnumbering the males.

The other native god is Paiawon, who represents an early stage in the evolution of the classical Greek Apollo, the sun god. In this early stage Paiawon or Paian is not only a sun god but also a god associated with the serpent—a connection we have seen before—and with healing of the sick. His healing function was later taken over by Asklepios, god of physicians, in classical times. Asklepios was said to be the son of Apollo, as is usual when one aspect of a god is split off to become a separate god. And both Apollo, the Pythian, and Asklepios are associated with the serpent. Apollo took over an older snake-goddess sanctuary at Delphi and reputedly slew the Python or serpent. Apollo's original sun-serpent aspect was apparently forgotten by classical times since myth has it that he slew the Python and assumed its oracular function at Delphi. With Asklepios the serpent fared better and as a consequence the medical profession honors the serpent to this day in its emblem of the Caduceus. Paiawon is, therefore, clearly the Cretan ancestor of classical Apollo.

The remaining two gods are Poseidon and Enyalios. Both are foreign imports. Poseidon was originally a god of the Thessalian Lapiths.[15] His traditional sphere was the sea, but he was also a horse-god and a god of springs and wells. He was definitely not of Minoan origin. His presence on the Linear B tablets points to the Greek speaking mainlanders who must have introduced him at Knossos. Enyalios means "battle god" and is probably an epithet for Ares, a war god of Thracian origin.[16] There can be no serious doubt that he, like Poseidon, and probably Athena, was brought in by the Mycenaeans who ruled at Knossos when the tablets were used.

There is also a reference to the "Priestess of the Winds" and to two sanctuaries, the "Daidaleion" and the "Labyrinthos." Reverence for the winds is not surprising on the sea-girt isle of Crete where a Bronze Age trading empire appears to have flourished. Merchant sailors and fishermen dependent upon sail and oar could hardly have failed to respect the winds of the sea. But it does not follow that the Winds here mentioned would mean a mere allegorical personification of natural forces. Myth reflects that the four cardinal Winds were under the sole direction of the Great Goddess until classical times.[17] That this was true at Knossos is confirmed by the fact that the tablet refers to a "Priestess of the Winds" not to a priest. The Winds came under a feminine deity represented by a feminine functionary.

According to one mythic tradition, Boreas, the North Wind, carried off Oreithuia, daughter of Erichthonius, the Pelasgian God of the Athenian Erectheum. And from information provided by Pausanias and Herodotus, it is evident that a sacred precinct in the Erectheum, which was barred to those who were not of the race of Erichthonius, contained four symbols representing the Sea, the Winds, Fire, and the Earth or the four elements.[18] This evidence points to a pre-Greek Pelasgian coupling of Boreas, and the other Winds, with Erichthonius, the Earth, for his name means "from the earth." In the Pythagorean number metaphysics, a geometrical pentad of five points arranged in a square with one point in the middle stood for the five elements—earth, air, fire, and water and the fifth essence or quintessence, spirit. The pentad was originally feminine and the element of air naturally included the Winds. Pythagoras derived this lore from the Orphics, who in turn derived it from Minoan religion. The sacred precinct in the Erectheum where the elements were united was presided over by Pelasgian Athena, the Great Goddess of Athens. Therefore, it is likely that the cult of the Winds, like the worship of Athena, was established in Athens before the arrival of the Greeks and that it had a counterpart in Knossos before the Greeks arrived there.

The sanctuaries called the Daidaleion and the Labyrinthos are mythically at home in Knossos where Daidalos, the artificer, was reputed to have built the Labyrinth for Minos and the Minotaur. We are obviously dealing here with a religious tradition of local origin.

The general picture which the Linear B tablets present of religion at Knossos at this time is clear enough to permit some inferences. It is evident that Minoan religious elements are very strong despite the presence of Greek speaking mainlanders. Goddesses of Minoan affinity clearly have a strong hold on the population at large if not on the Greek rulers as well. As Potnia Atana bears witness, these Mycenaean Greeks had probably adopted from their Pelasgian and other Aegean neighbors a religious outlook which permitted many parallels and identifications with the established divinities of Minoan Knossos.

This sort of parallelism among divinities is well illustrated by an incident in the Theseus myth. According to the myth, when Minos came to Athens to inspect the fourteen victims to be sent to Crete as tribute, Theseus boldly confronted him claiming that he was himself the son of Poseidon. Minos contemptuously tossed a golden ring into the sea and told Theseus to fetch it back from the realm of his father if he dared. Theseus dove into the sea and was carried by dolphins to the underwater abode of Poseidon and his goddess consort, Amphitrite. Amphitrite gave him a magic crown which subsequently lit his way in the Labyrinth. Theseus proved his claim by recovering the ring. But the interesting aspect of this story is that Theseus was provided with the means of surviving the ordeal of the Labyrinth not by Poseidon but by the feminine deity, Amphitrite. The sparkling crown she gave him and the ball of thread Ariadne gave him to survive the Labyrinth constitute a simple mythic equation. Minoan Ariadne and Athenian Amphitrite are clearly one Great Goddess under two different names.

However, in spite of certain identifications of this kind, the mainlanders also brought with them two aggressive male divinities of a quite different stamp, Poseidon, the "earth-shaker," and Enyalios, the war god.

Furthermore, Poseidon was evidently popular, for the tablets reveal four references to him, more than to any other divinity. Probably the religious situation at the time was in the nature of a tolerable compromise between the traditions of the rulers and the long established traditions of the ruled. At any rate, it is plain that the native Minoan traditions were not displaced. It appears rather that three foreign deities were simply added to a Minoan pantheon that had already developed a tendency toward polytheism.

The fission or splitting apart of the ancient Minoan Great Goddess, as well as of her sun-god consort, is already apparent in the group of divinities which may be assigned a strictly Cretan origin. The moon-goddess, whose number is five, is already visible as a pentad of five specialized goddesses who, nevertheless, reflect her five phases. Pipituna is her maiden phase, the new moon. Diwia is her bridal phase as wife of the sun-god. Hera is her central phase as full moon and mother. Eleuthia, the goddess as midwife, is her phase as waning moon—a goddess of autumnal age with a grown daughter. In short, the ancestor of the matronly Demeter with her grown daughter, Persephone. Demeter's sanctuary at Eleusis by the way reveals Demeter's connection with Eleuthia. And finally, Erinu is her fifth phase as hag, old moon, and bringer of death—later to become the classical Greek Erinys or Furies.

The same process can be observed in the two male sun-gods. Cretan Zeus appears to be the father of the younger Paiawon, whose serpent affinities connect him with serpent season on the calendar and accordingly with the rebirth of the sun at that time of the year. He is, therefore, the boy-sun as Pipituna is the maiden-moon. In classical times he becomes the young Apollo just as Pipituna becomes the virgin moon-goddess, Artemis. It is not an accident that in classical times Apollo and Artemis were paired brother and sister divinities.

Poseidon, Enyalios, and Athena are, of course, out of this picture since they are of Mycenaean development and were imported from the mainland. But the "potent one," the Mistress of the Labyrinth, has yet to be discussed. I suspect, because of her dominion over the Labyrinth, that all-inclusive symbol, she must be the Great Minoan Goddess herself—a still undivided unity transcending her temporal pentad. This interpretation certainly jibes with her significance in the labyrinth of the calendar, which as we have seen, is not remotely distant in time from the date of the Linear B tablets. But what would her name be at this time? If there is a kernel of historical truth in the myth of Theseus, her name must certainly be Ariadne.

And why not? According to myth, Theseus was a Mycenaean Greek hero born at Troezen in the Peloponnese and a son of the Athenian king, Aegeus.[19] We have seen that he also claimed descent from the horse-god Poseidon.[20] He went to Athens from Troezen after he had attained manhood and led the group of seven young men and seven maidens who were sent as tribute by the Athenians to King Minos of Crete. But with Ariadne's help he escaped alive from the Labyrinth after slaying the Minotaur. He rescued the youths and maidens and carried off his newfound love, Ariadne, whom the myth calls the daughter of King Minos. Later he abandoned Ariadne and she married Dionysos, who in his earliest form was a sun-god.

It is obvious that Theseus is not a strictly historical figure. On the contrary, he is a semi-divine hero and type of the sacred sun-king much like his earlier mythical predecessor, Herakles. Before his adventure in the Cretan Labyrinth he performed many miraculous feats, including significantly the capture of a dangerous bull at Marathon. But the myth is of Mycenaean origin in date and the adventure in Crete might well reflect Athenian contacts with Knossos in the period of the last prehistoric Palace.[21]

The fact that Theseus is the chief mythical hero of Athens and that the myth about his Cretan adventure dates from Mycenaean times appears interesting when we recall the picture presented by the Linear B tablets. Of course, the sanctuaries called the Daidaleion and the Labyrinthos connect with the myth. There are also other interesting connections. According to one tradition, Daidalos, after a falling out with Minos, took refuge in Athens and later assisted Theseus in a naval war which ended with the defeat and death of Minos in Sicily. This defeat in turn was followed up by a raid on Knossos and the capture of the Palace. The friendship of Daidalos and Theseus is understandable. Daidalos claimed descent from Erichthonius, the early Pelasgian god of pre-Greek Athens. The -*os* ending of his name is also evidence of his Pelasgian heritage. The Pelasgians were a minority group in Crete and were not unwilling to support the enemies of a ruling Minos. Hence, Athens is connected with Knossos by a link in the person of Daidalos.[22]

The three imported divinities who appear on the Linear B tablets are Potnia Atana (Athena), Poseidon, and Enyalios (Ares). All three forge links with Mycenaean Athens. The presence of Athena in this trio requires no comment. The presence of Poseidon is also significant. As we have seen, Theseus claimed descent from Poseidon. According to one myth, Poseidon was actually the father of Theseus, his alleged mortal father, King Aegeus of Athens, having been deceived by his wife Aethra.

Aethra, according to the myth, was a princess of Troezen. The Mycenaean priest-kings of Troezen claimed direct descent from Poseidon.[23] Aethra may have been the local name for the chief goddess at Troezen. Her union with Poseidon, the chief male divinity of the city, would then make mythic sense. The myth appears to reflect a royal marriage connecting the Athens of King Aegeus with the ruling dynasty of Troezen in the Peloponnese. Theseus, as the child of this marriage, may claim descent from Poseidon on his mother's side. The introduction of the cult of Poseidon at Athens may date, then, from the dynasty of Theseus.

The legends of Mycenaean date concerning the Erectheum on the Athenian acropolis are helpful. In that sanctuary Athena and

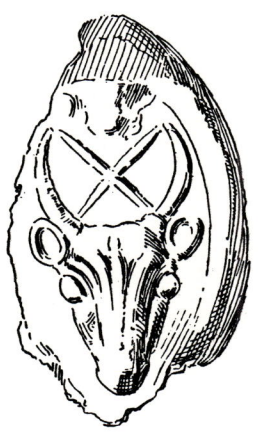

Figure 13
Middle Minoan III clay sealing from Knossos. HM. 152. Bucranium with cross and horns forming labrys motif.

Figure 14
Drawing of motif from clay sealing. From Zakros (c. 1700-1450 B.C.), HM. Gallery IX, Case 124.

Figure 15
Late Minoan Age seal from the Knossos district. AM. 1938.1070. Minotaur in circle of eternal return with eight-rayed sun disc emerging from bucranium. Above, a fertility bough.

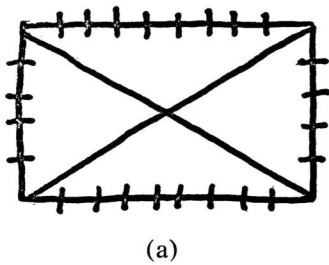

(a)

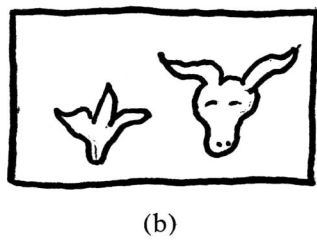

(b)

Figure 16
Engraving on seal from Knossos. Middle Minoan III, HM. Gallery II, Case 28, No. 1786. (a) Labyrinth motif with graduated marks on border. (b) Sacred lily at left and bucranium at right.

Figure 17
Engraving on seal from Crete. Late Minoan Age, HM. Gallery V,
Case 65, No. 2180. Labyrinth motif.

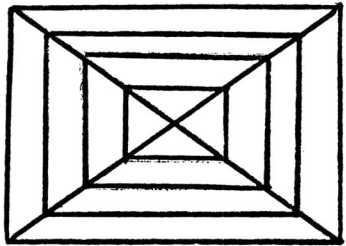

Figure 18
From the labrys (double axe) to the labyrinth. Related motifs from four Cretan seals. Middle Minoan III—Late Minoan Age. From Knossos and vicinity.

Figure 19 (a)
Flattened cylinder seal of banded agate. A Middle Minoan Age gem from Crete, AM. 1938.964. At left natural bands on agate suggest bull's horns. At right engraving shows bull-vaulter passing between horns of bull as bull enters labyrinth at lower left.

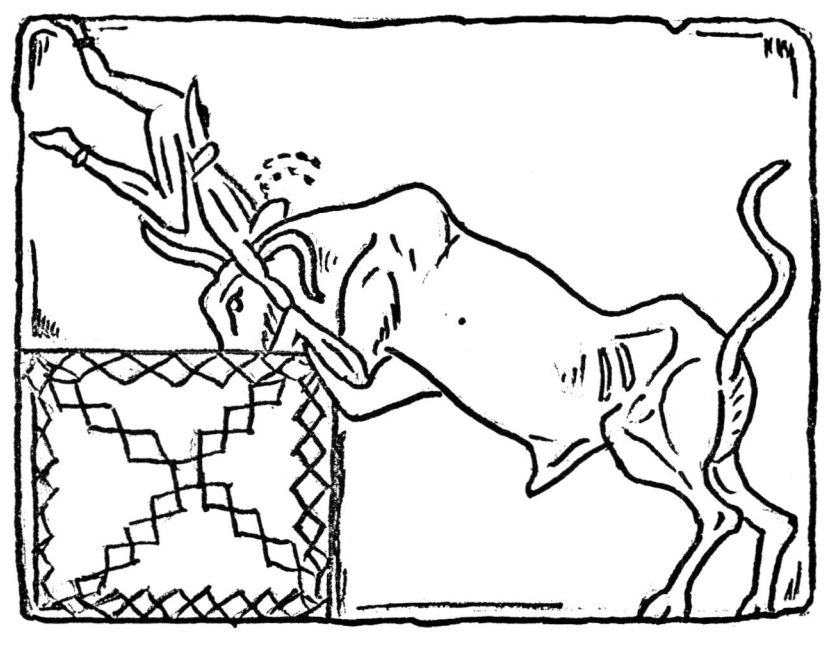

Figure 19 (b)

Figure 20
Labyrinth fresco in central court of Palace at Phaistos.

 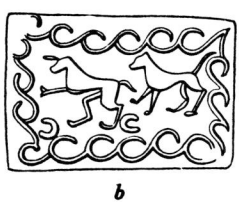

a *b*

Figure 21
Early Minoan Age ivory seal from Platanos, HM. 1044. (a) Amulet in shape of bull calf. (b) Bull and lion in moon-bordered labyrinth. New and old moon crescents in field.

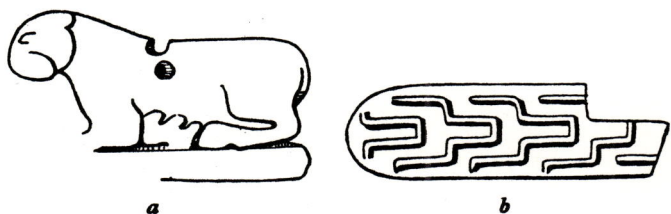

Figure 22
Early Minoan ivory seal from Kalathiana. HM. 821. (a) Amulet in shape of lion. (b) Stylized motif representing five phases of moon.

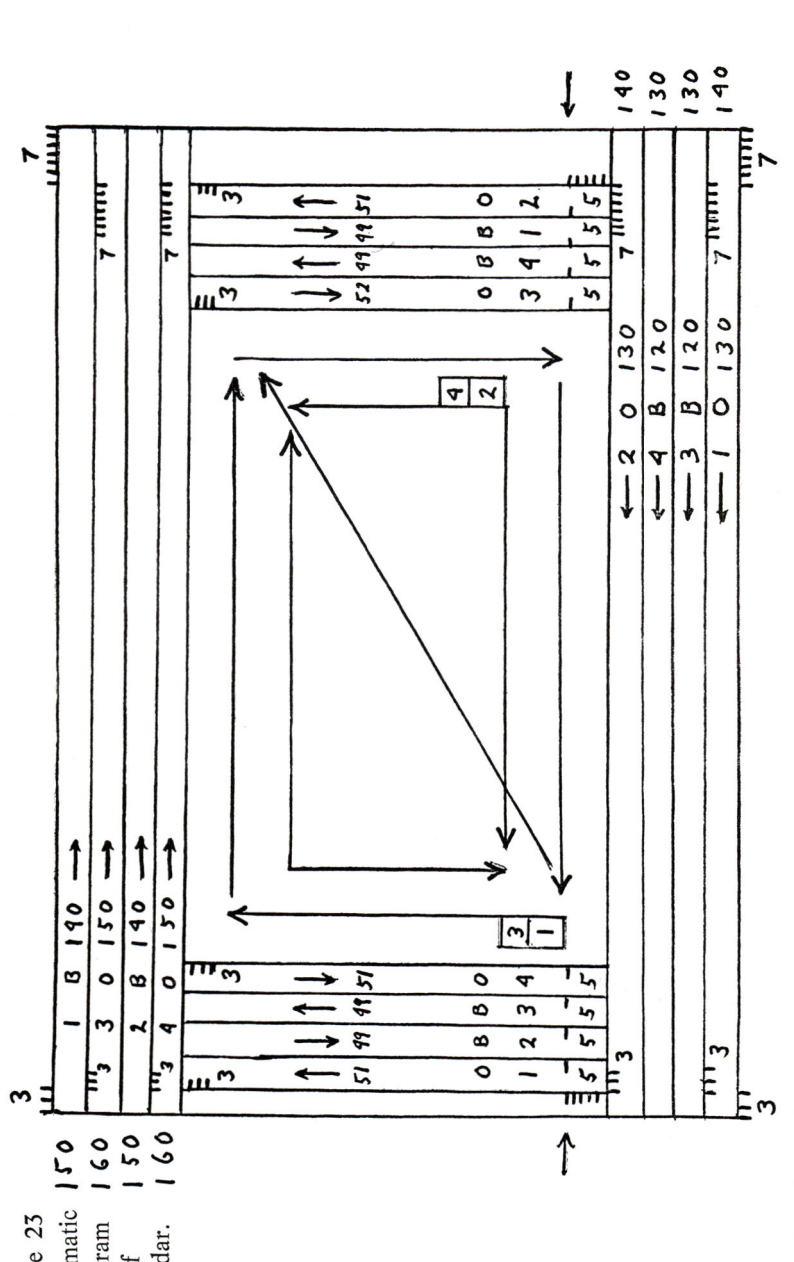

Figure 23 Schematic diagram of calendar.

Key

Years 1 and 3 begin at the arrow at left and years 2 and 4 at the arrow at right.—Year tracks are marked 1, 2, 3 and 4 and their color is indicated as B (blue) or O (orange).—Total days counted in any track indicated within the track.—Total number of marks on horizontal tracks indicated outside the appropriate tracks.—Number of days in festivals and where they fall indicated by graduated marks on appropriate tracks.—Arrows within frame indicate pattern of calendar sequence in four year cycle.

TABLE OF SEASONS AND FESTIVALS

Years 1 and 2			
Dates	Season Length	Dates	Festival Length
21 Dec.-2 Feb.	43 days-Winter	3 Feb.-5 Feb.	3 days-Spring Festival
6 Feb.-25 Jun.	140 days-Spring	26 Jun.-2 Jul.	7 days-Summer Festival
3 Jul.-30 Oct.	120 days-Summer	31 Oct.-2 Nov.	3 days-Fall Festival
3 Nov.-15 Dec.	44 days-Fall	16 Dec.-20 Dec.	5 days-Winter Festival

Years 3 and 4			
Dates	Season Length	Dates	Festival Length
21 Dec.-3 Feb.	44 days-Winter	4 Feb.-6 Feb.	3 days-Spring Festival
7 Feb.-26 Jun.	140 days-Spring	27 Jun.-3 Jul.	7 days-Summer Festival
4 Jul.-31 Oct.	120 days-Summer	1 Nov.-3 Nov.	3 days-Fall Festival
4 Nov.-15 Dec.	43 days-Fall 44 days-Fall (yr. 3-leap yr.)	16 Dec.-20 Dec.	5 days-Winter Festival

Figure 24

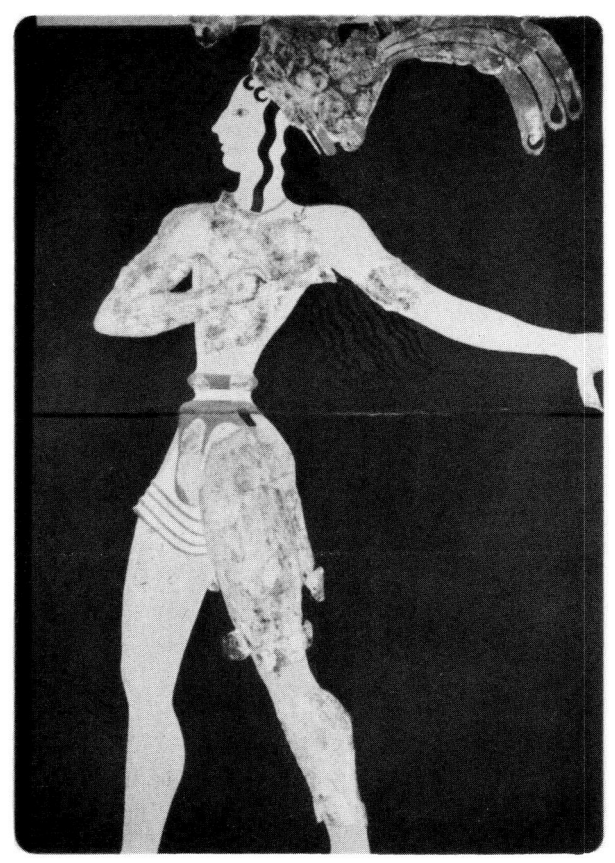

Figure 25
Priest-King relief fresco from Knossos.

Figure 26
Sketch of seal from Crete. Late Minoan Age. AM. 1941.120.
Goddess carrying sacrificed bull.

Figure 27
Sketch of seal design. From Knossos. Middle Minoan III. HM. 1597. This seal has a fourth face engraved with two standing birds. Illustration not available. Labyrinth motifs and serpent with cranes.

Erichthonius, both early Pelasgian divinities, were later forced to share honors with Poseidon. This probably means that when Theseus became king in Athens Poseidon had to be added to the cult of the earlier divinities, Athena and Erichthonius.[24]

The remaining foreign god on the Knossos tablets is Ares. Ares is also a god whose connection with Athens is very ancient. The sacred hill of Ares near the acropolis became in classical times the meeting place of the Areopagus, a kind of supreme court of Athens. But its sacred character has its roots in Mycenaean times. According to a tradition recorded on an inscription on the Parian Marble in classical times, Ares attended a court of judgment on this hill and the place of judgment received the name of Aeropagus as a consequence. The date of this mythical event is recorded on the Marble as in the reign of Cranaos at Athens. Cranaos is one of the earliest mythical kings of Athens following Cecrops, so the legend has almost certainly descended from Mycenaean times.[25]

It is evident, then that the links between Athens and Knossos at this period are many and that actual dynastic connections of some sort are indicated. Precisely what these connections were it is impossible to determine with certainty. But the Mycenaean Greeks of the Linear B tablets brought to Knossos divinities who were contemporaneously important in Athens. The legendary figure who appears as the love of Theseus in the Athenian myth of this date is Ariadne. Therefore, we may infer that the "Lady of the Labyrinth" mentioned on the Linear B tablets is certainly Ariadne.

The myth calls Ariadne the daughter of Minos. This may simply mean that an historical Athenian prince named Theseus was ceremonially married to a princess of Knossos whose royalty itself was derived from her ritual representation of the Goddess Ariadne just as Minos' royalty derived from his ritual representation of the sun-god. If so, Theseus would have had to slay the Minotaur at the summer festival marking the end of her father's 8 1/2 year reign, meaning that he may have sacrificed a consecrated bull or even that he may have killed the reigning king and inherited the throne through a sacred marriage with the princess. But of this we can know nothing with certainty. An historical Theseus and an historical Ariadne, named in honor of the goddess, may or may not have existed. But that the goddess, Ariadne, was the primary divinity of Knossos at this period is certain enough, and that is the significant point.

Ariadne was a moon-goddess with attributes of universal character. Her name means "Very Holy Maid."[26] She was also a vegetation and fertility goddess and the mate of the sun-god. But above all she was distinguished from the other divinities by virtue of being Mistress of the Labyrinth.

The evidence that she was Mistress of the Labyrinth is not confined to the Theseus myth alone. A coin of Knossos from the classical period (400 - 350 B.C.) shows her head surrounded by a labyrinthine meander frame.[27] This, of course, is late in date and reflects only a lingering memory of the distant past.

More significant is the tradition that she was honored by a labyrinthine ritual dance. In the *Iliad* Homer, describing the shield of Achilles, says that Hephaistos "wrought a dancing-floor like that which Daidalos once fashioned in spacious Knossos for Ariadne of the lovely hair. Youths and courted maidens were dancing on it, their hands on each other's wrists. The girls were wearing dresses of fine linen, the youths well-woven tunics with a faint gloss of oil; and the girls had lovely garlands, the youths golden daggers attached to their silver belts. Now they ran ever so lightly with cunning feet, as when a potter sits gripping his wheel with his hands and tries it out to see how it spins. Now again they ran in lines opposite to each other. A big crowd stood around enjoying the passionate dance; and two tumblers spun around in their midst setting the rhythm of the performance."[28] Homer's simile of the potter's wheel, spun clockwise, then counter-clockwise to try it out, is an apt description of a dance featuring spiralling in and spiralling out of a labyrinth and recalls the way the calendar is read. It is also, as Homer says, a courting dance suggesting the dance of the sun-god and the moon-goddess in the calendar cycle.

The scholiast explicating the passage in question says that Theseus, after escaping from the Labyrinth by means of Ariadne's clue, together with the rescued youths and maidens performed a spiralling dance for the gods that resembled his own entrance into and exit from the Labyrinth and that Daidalos showed them how to dance it. Lucian, too, throws light by listing Cretan dances as "Europa, Pasiphae, both the Bulls, the Labyrinth, Ariadne, Phaidra, Androgeos, Daidalos, Ikaros, Glaukos, the seer-craft of Polyidos, and Talos the bronze-sentinel of Crete."[29]

Plutarch gives us yet another clue. He says that after Theseus left Crete, he stopped at Delos where he dedicated an image of Aphrodite which he had received from Ariadne. He then danced with the young men a mimetic dance representing the circuit of the Labyrinth with measures involving turnings and returnings. This was called the Crane Dance and Theseus danced it around the Horned Altar.[30] It is plain that the Cypriot love goddess, Aphrodite, has been substituted here for her Minoan counterpart, the moon-goddess Ariadne. The crane, as we have previously seen, is one of the epiphanies of the Minoan goddess and the southern migration of the cranes coincides with the coming of fall as their northern migration would coincide with the coming of spring. Theseus danced around the Horned Altar which recalls the Minoan "horns of consecration" and the horns of the solar-lunar bull of the calendar. And since it is known that Delos was a center of a solar cult, we may hardly doubt that the dance here described is in honor of the sacred dance of the sun and the moon in the cycle of the calendar. It is a love dance which celebrates a sacred marriage.

It is evident, then, that Ariadne was a Cretan Goddess at the time of the Linear B tablets, and not a minor one, but the transcendant goddess of the Labyrinth, symbolized by the fresco calendar. She was goddess of life and death and of all the phases between, represented by the five moon-symbols of the calendar. She was spouse to the sun-god, but also his mother, his sister, and his eventual slayer. She not only stood for death in life, but also life in death, for her dying lover entered the clockwise spiral of death to emerge again through the counter-clockwise spiral of birth and regeneration.

There is good reason to believe that Ariadne promised her

lovers, the sacred kings, immortality. In the later Homeric tradition, the underworld of the dead is a dark and gloomy Hades from whence no one ever returned, except those intrepid visitors —Herakles, Theseus, Orpheus, and Odysseus—who like Dante descended and emerged again enlightened but still mortal. But there is also another classical Greek tradition of the Elysian Fields and the Islands of the Blessed. According to this tradition, not all, but certain heroes enjoyed an after life in an idyllic land beyond the Pillars of Hercules and far across the sea, where asphodel bloomed in fields perpetually mild and benign. This tradition is older and stems from Minoan and Mycenaean times. Glimpses of it, distorted by miscomprehension, come to us through some of the strange adventures of Odysseus in the *Odyssey*.

One is the detention of Odysseus by the demi-goddess Calypso on the island of Ogygia. She lives in a distant island far over the seas and she is enamoured of Odysseus and wishes to make him immortal. He, however, is impatient to return home and after Athena's intervention, Zeus sends Hermes to tell Calypso to release him. Here we have a distant island inhabited by a goddess of a superseded religion. Calypso is a daughter of the Titan, Atlas, one of the 'giants' ousted by the Olympian gods. She lives in a cave surrounded by a grove of trees. This suggests the cave cults of Crete and the sacred grove of an early fertility goddess. She wants Odysseus for her husband and promises to make him immortal. This means she wants to make him a sacred king, whereupon after his death he would become immortal. He has been with her for over seven years, and it is in the fateful eighth year that Hermes rescues him just in time. Hermes is traditionally the god who conducts the dead to the after-world, so it is not surprising that he should be sent to release Odysseus from Calypso's island. Although in the *Odyssey* Calypso is cast in the role of a mischievous enchantress, it is not difficult to see in her an echo of the prehistoric goddess who promises life after death to sacred kings in her mysterious island beyond the seas.

Another incident in the *Odyssey* with similar undertones is the adventure with the enchantress, Circe. She, too, lives on a distant island in the midst of a grove of trees. Once again it is Hermes who makes it possible for Odysseus to escape her enchantment—this time by providing him with a talisman in the form of a magic herb. She is described as a descendant of the sun-god, Helios, and Odysseus remains with her for precisely a solar year. When he does set forth with her blessing, he sails for the land of the dead with directions for entering and escaping that dread place provided by Circe's knowledge. Again we see clear indications of an ancient sun and fertility cult involving a dominant goddess, a mysterious island, a sacred grove, and an association of the goddess with life after death.

In the diverse myths of classical times concerning Ariadne, it is interesting that she is often reported to have left Crete and taken up residence on an island where she has also been thought to have died. The islands are various—Naxos, Cyprus, and the tiny island of Dia off the coast of Crete near Knossos. The islands suggest the Iles of the Blessed or the island of immortality. The tradition that she died on such an island may be interpreted as a mythic sign of the dying out of her cult. But I think it may also suggest that the island of immortality lies beyond the strictly mortal life. To pass to Ariadne's isle, the sacred king must first pass through the gates of death.

Now that we have a sharper focus on the prehistorical period to which the calendar fresco may be assigned, it should be possible to move inside the pillars of the fresco to see what secrets may be hidden at the very center of the Labyrinth.

NOTES

[1] Evans, *Palace of Minos*, Vol. III, p. 210.
[2] Evans, *Palace of Minos*, Vol. II. Supplementary Plate XIII, d and e; *P. M.*, Index Vol., p. 53.
[3] Evans, *Palace of Minos*, Vol. III, p. 210.
[4] For a complete discussion of the problem see William A. McDonald, *Progress Into the Past* pp. 383-403.
[5] Leonard R. Palmer, *A New Guide to The Palace of Knossos* (New York, 1969), p. 116.
[6] Palmer, *A New Guide to the Palace of Knossos*, p. 96 and p. 126.
[7] McDonald, *Progress Into the Past*, p. 330.
[8] Vermeule, *Greece in the Bronze Age*, p. 292.
[9] Vermeule, *Greece in the Bronze Age*, p. 293.
[10] Willetts, *Cretan Cults and Festivals*, pp. 168-172.
[11] Willetts, *Cretan Cults and Festivals*, pp. 197-198.
[12] Vermeule, *Greece in the Bronze Age*, p. 293.
[13] Angelo Procopiou, *Athens, City of the Gods* (New York, 1964), p. 51.
[14] Willetts, *Cretan Cults and Festivals*, pp. 199-220.
[15] Willetts, *Cretan Cults and Festivals*, p. 289.
[16] Willetts, *Cretan Cults and Festivals*, p. 186.
[17] Graves, *White Goddess*, p. 184.
[18] Procopiou, *Athens, City of the Gods*, p. 55.
[19] Martin P. Nilsson, *The Mycenaean Origin of Greek Mythology* (New York, 1963), p. 165.
[20] Procopiou, *Athens, City of the Gods*, p. 60.
[21] Nilsson, *The Mycenaean Origin of Greek Mythology*, p. 166.
[22] Procopiou, *Athens, City of the Gods*, p. 62.
[23] John Forsdyke, *Greece Before Homer* (New York, 1964), p. 47.

[24] Procopiou, *Athens, City of the Gods*, p. 52.
[25] Forsdyke, *Greece Before Homer*, p. 52.
[26] Willetts, *Cretan Cults and Festivals*, p. 193.
[27] Willetts, *Cretan Cults and Festivals*, p. 195.
[28] Willetts, *Cretan Cults and Festivals*, p. 123; quotation from *Iliad* of Homer.
[29] Willetts, *Cretan Cults and Festivals*, p. 124; quotation from Lucian.
[30] Willetts, *Cretan Cults and Festivals*, p. 124; paraphrase of Plutarch.

Chapter VIII

BEYOND THE PILLARS OF HERCULES

What are the Pillars of Hercules? Everyone knows the answer: the two rocky heights of Gibraltar and Ceuta on the Straits of Gibraltar, forming a gateway from the Mediterranean into the Atlantic. But I believe it can be shown that this is a popular error. Poseidonius, at any rate, thought this was a mistaken notion and held that they were the two pillars set up before the shrine of Hercules.[1]

We have already encountered Hercules or Herakles as a sun-hero of Cretan origin and leader of the Dactyls as well as mythical founder of the Olympic Games. Mythic stories about him abound but many are later accretions. His adoption as the mythical hero of Mycenaean Tiryns and Thebes is a development which post-dates his Cretan origin. In his earliest guise he is a type of the sacred sun-king and a principal in a mimetic ceremony of initiation for youths and maidens of marriageable age. In this ritual he is, together with his twin, a leader of a band of twelve celebrants.[2] Despite the later traditions of his birth, his mother was Cretan Hera, and as we have seen Hera was the representative of the Great Goddess as mother and full moon in the period of the calendar fresco.

In classical times artistic representations of Herakles show him to be a muscular, bull-necked athlete wearing a lion's skin and carrying a club. The club is of oak and it is a remnant of a primitive stage of his cult when, in northern Greece, he was a sacred oak-king of the year. What is significant about this early stage is the fact that he was one of the two twin kings of the solar year. In Minoan tradition these twins are represented by two calendar beasts, the bull and the lion. The

104

Minotaur, with a man's body and a bull's head, represents a transitional stage in a change from theriomorphic to anthropomorphic symbolism. Herakles, who is represented as entirely human, nevertheless retains the bull-neck and bulky build of the solar bull with which he coalesced when as solar oak-king he was equated with solar bull-king. Such twin kings—and there are many of the kind in mythology—always have a contrasting brother distinguished in some particular manner so that the twins may be told apart and associated with specific seasons of the year. The lion skin of Herakles serves this purpose. According to myth one of the Twelve Labours of Herakles was the slaying of a lion and he retained the skin as his trophy. The twin of the Minoan calendar bull, of course, is the lion.

It is not a meaningless coincidence that Herakles performed precisely twelve great Labours. As we have noticed in the numerical symbolism of the calendar, twelve alternates with eleven as a season number. Twelve is the number of Herakles, the bull of the spring season, while eleven is the number of his twin, the lion of the summer season. In one of his twelve Labours, Herakles slew the Nemean lion, but in another of these Labours he captured the Cretan bull.[3] He assumes, therefore, the functions of both twins—being both lion slayer and bull fighter. But the bull-lion circle is really a unity in any case, so Herakles may subsume both functions alternately. His number is therefore twelve in spring and eleven in summer. And he and his twin are the leaders of the band of twelve in the initiation and sacred marriage rites discussed in Chapter VI.

It is significant that the last two Labours of Herakles, the eleventh and twelfth, are both adventures which take place in a mythic setting symbolic of life after death. This is not true of any of the other Labours. The eleventh Labour carried him to the utmost boundary of the world, the fabled Garden of the Hesperides, which is another version of the Isles of the Blessed or the Elysian Fields where a chosen few enjoy a life of eternal bliss. It has already been shown that this idea is a Minoan heritage and that Ariadne is the goddess specifically associated with it. In his twelfth Labour, Herakles goes to the

Underworld of the dead and brings back the guardian dog, Cerberus. The idea of the Underworld is indeed Greek, but the conception of a mortal returning from that world is not. It implies that Herakles defeated death itself. It is most appropriate that these should be his last two Labours and that they are canonically so is certainly not accidental.

But why should he have to overcome death twice? The logical answer is that he and his twin both did so. The question that arises next is: Who is this missing twin? There ought to be a mythic figure who corresponds with the calendar beast, the lion, as Herakles corresponds with the bull. Theseus comes to mind because his mythic feats so closely parallel those of Herakles. But the fact is that the Theseus myth is slightly later in date than the core of the Herakles cycle and parallels it largely because in its miraculous aspects it was modeled on the Herakles cycle.[4] So we shall have to reject Theseus for this role.

The difficulty in finding the proper candidate stems from the fact that what we know of the Herakles myth comes to us in the shape it was given by the Mycenaeans of Tiryns and Thebes. In Crete Herakles must have been a ritual figure representing a bull-king of the year and the leader of the Dactyls in calendric festival games. The Mycenaeans converted him into an individualistic folk hero. Thus he has no twin in Mycenaean tradition and his original relationship to Cretan Hera, as son and lover, is distorted so that he becomes the unloved step-son of Olympian Hera.

Nevertheless, there is in Pindar's "Ode to the Infant Herakles," written in 476 B.C. for Chromius of Syracuse, who claimed descent from Herakles, a passage recalling an old tradition that Herakles had a twin brother. Pindar writes, "once, men say, that son of Zeus [Herakles] with his twin brother came straight from his mother's womb of suffering into the wonder of the radiant day. . . ."[5] Pindar does not identify the twin by name, but it is clear that he is not referring to Iphicles, the reputed half brother of Herakles, since the reference is to a natural twin. In classical tradition the identity of the twin has been lost.

We must go to Crete to find the lost twin. And there we find a mythic figure whose outline is only faintly discernible from a few remaining cryptic references, but who, nevertheless, fits the role. We came across a reference to him earlier in Lucian who lists among Cretan dance-themes a dance called "Talos the bronze-sentinel of Crete."[6]

The information available from ancient sources on Talos is mostly fragmentary and enigmatic. We find that he was identified with the Phoenician Kronos, who like the Cretan Minotaur, had a bull's head. He is also described as "the bronze man" and he belonged to the bronze generation. He was also said to be the sun, a conception which appears to relate to his bronze color. But there also appears to be some sense in which he was supposed to have been made of metal, for it is said that Hephaistos made him or Hephaistos gave him to Minos. Another tradition tells us that he was a fertility god and that on his death he was transformed into a partridge, a bird associated with fertility. The Athenian version is that he was thrown from a height by Daidalos and transformed by Athena into a partridge in mid air. One puzzling attribute is that he was accounted a guardian, "running round the island of Crete three times a day."[7] And even more strange is the report that a single vein extended from his neck to his ankles and the vein was stopped by a bronze nail. It is also a part of mythic tradition that Medea killed him by driving a pin in his heel. He was the mythical inventor of compasses for drawing circles true and also of the potter's wheel. Simonides tells us that he sprang into a fire. Finally, in classical times in Crete he became identified with Zeus as Zeus Tallaios, and from one recorded donation to him, he appears to have been a patron of physicians.[8]

At first sight these varied reports of the mythographers appear to present a chaotic picture of which little can be made. But a closer inspection reveals a mythic consistency which is readable. Of first importance is to note that he was a sun-hero associated with male fertility. These attributes as well as his connection with a bull-god parallel Herakles as sun-hero and bull. As a patron of physicians he also ties in with the solar serpent as healer. That he is a dying sun-hero indicates that he is one of the twin solar kings of the year just as Herakles is. Again like Herakles he appears to have overcome death. In one myth he is preserved from death by Athena who transforms him into a partidge in mid air. Another version is that he leaped into a fire. But this also parallels the Herakles myth, for the last deed of Herakles was to build a pyre on Mount Oeta where he achieved apotheosis and immortality by leaping into it.[9] There was a Cretan dance named after him which suggests the ritual dances and games led by Herakles and his twin at calendric celebrations of the sacred marriage and the initiation of youths and maidens.

In all these respects Talos resembles Herakles closely enough to be his twin. Such mythic twins, however, are usually distinguishable as well as equatable. The distinguishing aspect of Talos is that he is associated with the lame smith-god, Hephaistos, and with the artificer, Daidalos. Both Hephaistos and Daidalos were patrons of metal workers, and in the Bronze Age, this would have meant the working and casting of bronze. Talos is said to have been a bronze man and to have had a single vein extending from his neck to his ankles stopped by a bronze nail. R. F. Willetts points out that this has been interpreted as a mythic reflection of the *cire-perdue* method of bronze-casting.[10] Molten bronze was poured into a mold of a statue at the top and permeated the mold melting away a layer of wax which drained off at the bottom and a projecting nipple of bronze at the extremity, much like a bronze nail, was filed off of the statue after the bronze had hardened. A bronze statue of Talos could have been so made. If so, a skilled craftsman would have made such a statue in the name of the patron god of smiths, who was later called Hephaistos in Greece but who appears to have been Talos himself in Mycenaean Crete.

This part of the myth could well have a second but not contradictory meaning. Hephaistos, like Talos, was thrown from a height. The injury incurred in his fall, made one leg lame so that he limped or hobbled when he walked. Now it happens that sacred kings with one lame foot or a vulnerable foot are common enough to be a type in mythology. One example is OEdipus, king of Thebes, whose ankle was pierced in childhood to secure him when he was abandoned by his royal parents. The name OEdipus means "lame foot." Another, of course, is Achilles whose goddess mother, Thetis, dipped him in fire to make him immortal, but who in the process held him by the heel and failed to complete the job so that his heel alone remained vulnerable. The mythical lameness of Hephaistos is of the same sort in significance. It is also worth noting that Hephaistos was the consort of the pre-Greek fertility goddess of Cyprus, Aphrodite. Aphrodite was the Cypriot name of the Great Goddess who was worshipped throughout the eastern Mediterranean under different appellations. Talos is also a sacred sun-king associated with metal working and also with a vulnerable heel. The tradition that Medea killed him by driving a pin in his heel makes sense in this light. And, hence, the story of a bronze nail in his ankle has a second meaning not contradictory to the one previously discussed but enriching it by supplementation.

It is perhaps not superfluous to add that the mythic archetype of the lame artificer hero may be a psychologically significant image of the artist as a human type. He carries with him through life a childhood injury of some kind—physical or psychic— which is the source of his compensating drive to excell in an area beyond the reach of the more simply adjusted ordinary man. He is vulnerable, but this Achilles heel is also the source of his strength. The blindness of Homer, Milton, and Joyce, the deafness of Beethoven, the crook-back of Pope and the lameness of Byron are all historical examples of this principle in action.[11]

Talos is the twin of the muscular athlete, Herakles. He is much like Herakles as we have seen. Both are archetypal sun-heroes dedicated ultimately to the Great Goddess, the source of creation and vitality. But they differ in an interesting complementary way. Herakles is a type of the hero as man of action and his realm is the obective physical world as his season is the time of the waxing sun. Talos is a type of the hero as man of technical skill and art and his realm is the subjective world of thought as his season is the time of the waning sun. Both these types are ultimately one in universal human nature, but it is their fate to destroy each other alternately in the cyclical temporal world. Talos, the summer lion of the calendar, must kill Herakles, the spring bull, at the summer solstice, but Herakles must kill him in turn at the winter solstice. The bull-lion circle thus thrives upon itself.

A few attributes of Talos remain unexplained. His reputed invention of the potter's wheel and of the compass are not difficult to understand. As a patron of craftsmen it would be natural to credit him with the invention of these important tools. Perhaps also there is a connection between the circular image of the sun, which he represents, and the circular potter's wheel as well as with a tool, the compass, which enables one to draw perfect circles. But the tradition that he was a sentinel "running round the island of Crete three times a day" remains a mystery. I suspect that the reference may have something to do with a device for time keeping, dividing a day into six four-hour units, but this can not be proven. However, I think we may be reasonably sure that we have properly identified Talos as the solar-twin of Herakles and as the lion who annually slays the bull.

But what are the Pillars of Hercules which Poseidonius claimed stood before the shrine of the apotheosized hero? To answer the question we must look into the significance of pillars in general in Minoan religion. Sir Arthur Evans was convinced that sacred pillars and pillar shrines were an important element in Minoan religion and that *baetyls* or sacred stones were closely related to sacred trees.[12] Sir James George Frazer had earlier shown the connection between groves of sacred trees and ancient fertility cults in general in the *Golden Bough*. Robert Graves has significantly added to our knowledge of this subject by his study of the symbolic connotations of sacred trees and pillars in relation to the calendar and the alphabet in various prehistoric cultures of Europe and Asia.[13] These studies, although they are not specifically focused on our problem, provide insights that are helpful. At the very least, they make us aware that pillars upholding a lintel appearing in a religious context as a motif in Minoan art probably have more than a merely utilitarian architectural reference.

We have previously seen that Herakles was, in a primitive stage of his cult, an oak-king of the year and that in many classical representations he carries an oak club. According to Robert Graves the twin of Herakles in ancient Celtic poetic tradition was a holly or hollyoak-king of the waning year who would seem to parallel the Cretan Talos. But the northern holly is not a tree of Crete. What tree was associated with Talos in Crete I have not been able to discover, but I venture the suggestion that it may have been the laurel. The laurel like the holly is evergreen and it was later the sacred tree associated with the sun god, Apollo, at his oracle at Delphi on Mount Parnassos. The priestesses of the oracle chewed laurel leaves to induce a prophetic trance. Furthermore, Apollo took over the function of Talos in classical times as the patron god of the arts and the awarding of a laurel wreath to winners of poetic contests was traditional.

It is interesting that the victor in the Olympic Games in classical times was crowned with an olive wreath. There is also a legend that the Kouretes, who as we have seen are equatable with the Dactyls, came from Crete to Olympia and there ran a race, the winner being crowned with wild olive.[14] Herakles, the leader of the Dactyls and mythic founder of the Olympic Games, was probably not associated with the oak in Crete but with the wild olive. The oak, in most of its varieties, is a northern tree. On the other hand, the cultivation of the olive in Crete goes back to Minoan times as the great jars for the storage of olive oil found at the Palace of Knossos attest. Indeed, the agricultural economy of Crete to this day rests primarily upon the production of olive oil. The conclusion to be drawn is that in Minoan Crete the sacred tree of Herakles was the olive and that later, when his cult was adopted in more northern climes, it became the oak.

The earliest version of an iconographic motif which might be called the Pillars of Hercules was probably two sacred trees—the olive and the laurel, each representative of a different aspect of creative fertility—standing before an open air shrine dedicated to Herakles and his twin, Talos. A natural enough later development would be to construct an edifice entered between two wooden pillars of the appropriate wood, upholding a lintel and perhaps also a simple pediment.

There is good evidence that such shrines existed in Minoan Crete. The shrine motif appears frequently on talismanic gems of the Late Minoan Age. These talismanic stones are usually almond-shaped and pierced with a string-hole for wearing about the neck. They obviously have religious significance since they were worn as talismans. Their almond-shape is a fertility reference since the almond is a seed and the almond tree grows prolifically in Crete.

Let us look at some examples. The first is a stone in the Ashmolean from East Crete dated Late Minoan II (A.M. 1938. 984). The engraving shows a rustic shrine fronted by two tree-trunk pillars with a threshold below, a lintel above, and a simple wooden pediment. (Fig. 30) Within the shrine is an egg-shaped baetylic stone pierced by a slanting member that could hardly have anything other than phallic significance. The shrine is surmounted by two serpents, one on each side.

The following points should be noted. The twin pillars of the shrine are unfinished posts retaining their branches and revealing their derivation from living sacred trees. The baetylic stone within is egg-shaped. It thus symbolically bridges the gap between inanimate stone and living organisms, such as trees or animals, because from such a stone-like shell life is hatched. It is certainly a feminine emblem and the piercing member is as obviously masculine. The combination clearly suggests generation and birth or, since this is a shrine and in a sense a tomb, rebirth after death. The twin serpents complement the twin pillars and are male symbols of the two halves of the sun's serpent season which, as we have seen, is the time of the death of the waning sun and of the rebirth of the waxing sun. The Pindaric Ode to the infant Herakles, previously mentioned, tells how Hera in a fit of jealousy sent two serpents to destroy Herakles and his twin at the child bed of Alcmene, the mortal woman supposed to have been the mother of Herakles by Zeus in classical tradition. This is an evident inversion of the original significance of the two serpents, who in Minoan religion were the benevolent agents of birth, not death, and Hera herself in Minoan tradition would have been the mother of the twins and beloved by the serpents. The conclusion is that this motif represents a shrine of the two solar twins of the year who at this period in Crete were probably called Herakles and Talos.

Another example is a talismanic stone from Siteia in the Ashmolean dated from the same period (A.M. 1938. 985). It is engraved with a similar shrine motif. (Fig. 31) The pediment of the shrine is made of rustic wood, but an interesting variation is that the twin pillars as well as the baetylic pillar within appear to be of stone. Here we have made a transition from sacred trees to sacred stone pillars and we are already on the road which will eventually lead to the columned portico of a classical Greek temple. At the left, however, is a tree or branch in foliage to remind us of the derivation of the pillar from the sacred living tree. At the right is a chevron design of problematical significance, but possibly having a feminine genital reference. Below the shrine is a wooden structure which V. E. G. Kenna suggests is an altar, the shrine itself being a small model thus displayed.[15] The parallel significance of this engraving and the former one is obvious.

A third example of this motif is on a gold signet ring from Knossos in the Ashmolean dated Late Minoan II. (A.M. 1938. 1127). The design displays a shrine with a two-pillar entrance. (Fig. 32) Both of the pillars and the shrine itself appear to be made of stone. Within stands a baetylic pillar with a capital and base. Above the stone structure sacred trees remind us again of the symbolic origin of the stone pillars. In the courtyard stands a single tapering pillar with four rings about the base. To the left of this pillar a scene of religious import is enacted. A female figure in a Minoan flounced skirt with a sacral knot behind her back holds up her arms in a gesture of mourning. She is probably a priestess representing the goddess since below her are five vertical bars recalling the moon-goddess' number.

The one for whom she mourns is the young sun-king whose figure is shown holding a rod or sceptre as he ascends (or does he hang?) beside the tapering pillar. The pillar has four rings at its base which is his number and together with the five vertical bars below the priestess the number becomes nine which represents the years of his reign. Surrounding his head, or rather his neck to be more exact, is an elliptical arrangement of a bead-like character. Some interpreters have thought this to be a nimbus. Perhaps they are right. However, since there are exactly eight of these objects, arranged like beads on a string, and they appear to encircle his neck, I am inclined to interpret this as the eight-beaded necklace of a sacred priest-king. As we have seen, the figure in the priest-king relief fresco wears a similar necklace which is probably emblematic of the eight-year cycle of the calendar. At the far left are rocks and shrubs suggesting the goddess' dominion over stone and plant alike. Finally, the two pillars of the shrine are marked by eight and seven stone blocks respectively, which corresponds with the eight and seven moon symbols alternately used on the vertical pillars of the calendar in any single year.

This signet ring enlarges the significance of the twin pillar shrine motif. It now appears that the shrine is also the tomb of a sacred sun-king who dies in the ninth year following an eight year term just as the calendar indicates. The two pillars at the entrance of the shrine reveal his dual nature in any single year and the alternating eight and seven-stoned pillars tie in with the pillars of the calendar fresco. The calendar itself is, therefore, a variation on the pillar shrine, having not only upright columns but also a threshold and a supported lintel. And since the shrine is also a tomb, the calendar pillars take on the additional significance of a gateway to the after-life.

We may now answer the question with which we began: What are the Pillars of Hercules? Poseidonius was right in asserting that they were the pillars before the shrine of Hercules. But the full meaning of this assertion appears to have been lost in his time. The true Pillars of Hercules were not the dumb stone columns of a particular local sanctuary dedicated to Hercules any more than they were the heights at the Straits of Gibraltar, although both of these errors are not without a limited truth. As it has been shown, the true Pillars of Hercules are in essence an emblem or artistic image with multiple connotations. But above all—or rather transcending all—they represent the gates of the world which lies beyond death. It is true that the Elysian Fields or Garden of the Hesperides or Island of Ariadne—call it what you will—was, as tradition said, beyond the Pillars of Hercules, but not on a physically existing island beyond the Straits of Gibraltar, which was considered the boundary of the known world in classical times. The Pillars of Hercules marked the gate to the Labyrinth, the gate to death, and the gate to life after death.

And now we may return to the myth that Herakles twice defeated death in his eleventh and twelfth Labours—he and his twin, Talos. These two mythic events are supplemented by the tradition that Herakles built a funeral pyre on Mount Oeta which consumed his mortal self and released his immortal self apotheosized among the gods. A third mythic event related of Herakles is even more pertinent in supporting the conclusion at which we have arrived. This Homeric myth tells how Herakles confronted Hades himself, the god of the Greek Underworld, and wounded him with an arrow and put him to flight. The place where the combat occurred is quite significant in the light of the argument expounded above. It took place "in the Gate, among the Dead."[16] In other words, Herakles' victory over death took place between the "Pillars of Hercules" as the entrance to the Underworld came to be called after this extraordinary victory. For it *was* an extraordinary victory in the eyes of the classical Greeks who believed in general that death was final and that immortality was only for the gods. In the classical Greek view, Herakles, a mortal man who achieved immortality, is the exception not the rule. The exception exists only because Herakles is a mythic figure surviving from the prehistoric religion of Minoan Crete and its counterparts on the mainland in Mycenaean times.

We have discovered, then, that the pillars of the calendar

fresco are symbolic of the Pillars of Hercules and that to go beyond them means to enter the Labyrinth, an emblem of the Underworld of the dead. Virgil was clearly aware of the significance of the Labyrinth as an emblem of the Underworld. In Book VI of the *AEneid*, his Trojan hero, Aeneas, faces his final and culminating trial. The final trial—true to mythic archetype—is a mission to the dreaded and mysterious Underworld where he will be enlightened by the shade of his dead father, Anchises, and return from thence, as if reborn, to fulfill his destiny by founding Rome. When he arrives at the gates of the Underworld, the pillars through which he must pass are described by Virgil in detail. We are told they were carved in relief by none other than Daidalos and the motif represented was the Cretan Labyrinth. The symbolic equation is unmistakable. The Labyrinth equals the Underworld. At the very center of the Labyrinth lies death, but, as the Herakles myth reveals, there also lies Ariadne's island or a life transcending death. The Labyrinth is also, therefore, a memory of the womb, viewed psychologically, or, mythically viewed, the mystic womb of the Great Goddess from whence such favored sons as Herakles, Theseus, Orpheus, Odysseus and Aeneas emerge reborn. And now, at last, we are equipped with a symbolic understanding of the labyrinth motif that should permit us to interpret the bull-vaulting scene in the center of the labyrinth of the calendar.

NOTES

[1] Graves, *White Goddess*, p. 247.

[2] Originally, in Crete, Herakles appears to have been one of the ten Dactyls, the leader associated with the phallic thumb. But just as in the development of Greek drama, the principals or actors were separated from the chorus, so Herakles and his twin were separated from the ten Dactyls as principals in the earlier ritual and the total number was increased from ten to twelve. The parallel drawn here with Greek drama is not without significance, for the Minoan bull ritual of Herakles and his antagonist twin appears to have been a predecessor of the Greek goat ritual of Dionysos and an antagonist, which developed into Greek tragedy.

[3] Nilsson, *The Mycenaean Origin of Greek Mythology*, p. 213.

[4] Nilsson, *The Mycenaean Origin of Greek Mythology*, p. 164.

[5] Pindar, *The Oxford Book of Greek Verse in Translation*, ed., T. F. Higham and C. M. Bowra (Oxford, 1944), transl. by C. J. Billson, p. 317.

[6] Willetts, *Cretan Cults and Festivals*, p. 124.

[7] Willetts, *Cretan Cults and Festivals*, p. 101.

[8] Willetts, *Cretan Cults and Festivals*, p. 249.

[9] Nilsson, *The Mycenaean Origin of Greek Mythology*, p. 199.

[10] Willetts, *Cretan Cults and Festivals*, p. 101.

[11] It is interesting that James Joyce identified himself with Daidalos in his *Portrait of the Artist as a Young Man* and *Ulysses*.

[12] Sir Arthur Evans, "The Mycenaean Tree and Pillar Cult," *Journal of Hellenic Studies*, 1901, *passim*.

[13] Graves, *White Goddess, passim*.

[14] Willetts, *Cretan Cults and Festivals*, p. 210.

[15] Kenna, *Cretan Seals*, p. 126.

[16] Nilsson, *The Mycenaean Origin of Greek Mythology*, p. 203.

Chapter IX

THE TRAGIC GAMES OF LOVE AND DEATH

What is the significance of the bull-vaulting scene in the center of the fresco calendar? (Plate II) The first and most obvious answer is that it is an athletic spectacle. But why should an acrobatic sport or game appear as a motif in the center of a calendar designed primarily for ritual purposes? Here again we need not look far for an obvious answer. The sport itself is not a secular amusement—at least not in origin—but part of a ritual. Moreover, the ritual might reasonably be expected to be a periodic one performed on a festival determined by the calendar.

The Olympic Games on the Peloponnese will provide us with some valuable clues. The Games of classical times clearly originated as part of a religious ritual at a sanctuary, and they were held every four years in celebration of a calendar festival. As almost everyone knows, the classical Greeks reckoned historical dates in terms of Olympiads or four-year periods beginning with the date of the celebration of the Olympic Games in 776 B.C. This is the date of the first recorded Olympiad.

The sanctuary itself is far more ancient. I have visited the excavations at Olympia. The remains of prehistoric structures there indicate that it was a sanctuary dedicated to a female deity in Mycenaean times long before Olympian Zeus was installed as patron. There are remains of early temples dedicated to Rhea and Hera, both goddesses of Cretan origin. Even in classical times the presiding dignitary was a Priestess of Demeter. According to tradition the most ancient event in the Games was a race involving fifty young priestesses of Hera for the privilege of becoming the new Chief Priestess.[1] The practice of sacrificing a black bull at the central altar of the sanctuary continued as late as the second century A.D. when the wife of Herodes Atticus was Chief Priestess. The bull suggests a connection with the solar-bull of the Knossos calendar and with Herakles as king of the waxing year. The myth which credits Herakles and the Dactyls with the transplantation of the games from Crete makes sense in terms of the pre-classical character of the Olympic sanctuary. The pre-classical games apparently were in honor of a fertility goddess, engaged female as well as male competitors, and were related to the solar year through Herakles and the bull.[2]

A myth of Mycenaean date localized at Olympia throws additional light on the original nature of the games held there. According to the myth, Pelops, for whom the Peloponnese is named, won his kingdom by marrying the daughter of an earlier king. Suitors of the princess were obliged to compete with her royal father in a chariot race. If the suitor could win, the prize was the princess and the kingdom. If not, he paid a price, his life. Many suitors competed and lost their lives. The princess found Pelops interesting and connived, with the help of her father's charioteer, who weakened the axle of the king's chariot, to cause his wreck and death and to insure a victory for Pelops who won princess and kingdom both. The myth reflects a ritual athletic competition which leads to a marriage, a funeral, and a change in kingship through matrilinear succession.

The Homeric poems and other early epic cycles also tell us something about the significance of ritual games in Mycenaean times. The games in the Homeric and other early poems are either funeral games or wedding games. That is they are celebrated at the funeral of a king in his honor or as a contest of some kind leading to the winning of a bride or a husband. A number of obvious examples come to mind. There are the funeral games in honor of Patroclos in the *Iliad,* and the games at the funeral of Achilles in the *Aithiopis* of Arctinos of Miletos.[3] In the *Odyssey* the suitors of Penelope are challenged to an archery contest to win her hand. Odysseus' revenge on them precludes a wedding, but nevertheless a winning of Penelope by contest was in the offing. Also in the *Odyssey* are the Phaiacian games at the court of Alcinoos in which Odysseus competes. Strictly speaking, we have no wedding here either, but it is perfectly clear that the princess Nausicaa sees in Odysseus a potential husband. It is likely that Homer adapted to his purposes an older tale that ended in a wedding for the victor.

The conclusions to be drawn from the accumulated evidence are that ritual games in Mycenaean times were celebrated in connection with funeral and marriage rites, with the transfer of kingship through matrilinear succession, with a solar fertility cult, with worship of a supreme feminine deity, and at Olympia at least, with Herakles, with the sacrifice of a bull, and with a four year calendar cycle. These factors taken together point to the Minoan origin of such games and to the bull-vaulting sport of the Knossos calendar as a related ritual.

As we have previously seen, Herakles and his twin, Talos, were the principals in a calendric festival involving a celebration of the sacred marriage of the sun-god and the moon-goddess and the initiation of marriageable aged youths and maidens into adult social status.[4] R. F. Willetts has shown that such initiation ceremonies in Crete and on the mainland were still practiced in classical times and that they usually involved an ordeal in the form of an athletic contest. According to Willetts these rituals originated in Minoan Crete and are related to the bull games depicted on many works of Minoan art.[5] We have, then, established clear connections between the bull-vaulting scene on the fresco calendar and ritual games with specific reference to marriage and to funeral rites.

Now let us look closely at the fresco picture. (Plate II) The first observation is that the two figures at the left and right are maidens while the central vaulting figure is a young man. This is evident because the central figure is red, the color males are always rendered in Minoan art, while the other two figures are white, the conventional color for rendering females. Moreover, the figure on the right displays a bared bossom. We see, then, that both youths and maidens participated in this sport. We should also note that red is the color of the sun-god and white the color of the moon-goddess. The ritual depicted, then, may be expected to have a reference to both deities.

The charging bull is rendered in four colors—brown, white, ochre, and black. Four is the sun-king's number. The background against which he is set off is blue like the sky in which the sun shines. He appears, then, to be a solar-bull, but since his horns are crescent-shaped, he is also related to the moon. Another observation is that the maiden on the right, who appears about to catch the vaulting youth, has her wrists bound with a red tape—five bands on one wrist and four on the other for a total of nine bands. Nine, of course, is the number of the year in which the sacred sun-king's term comes to an end, as we have seen. It is evident, then, that we have symbolic references to both the sun and the moon and to the ninth year following the completion of an eight year solar-lunar cycle.

The next observation is that the three figures form a dynamic sequence indicating the three phases in the movement of the vaulting youth. First he must grasp the horns of the bull in the manner of the figure at the left. Then he passes through the horns in a somersault over the bull's back represented by the central figure. Finally, he alights on his feet behind the bull with arms outstretched for balance as suggested by the figure on the right.

The question that interpreters of this scene usually ask is: Can such an acrobatic feat actually be performed? I think this is the wrong question to ask. First, because it can not be answered with much certainty. Secondly, because it is an irrelevant question at best. I believe the proper question to ask is: What is the ritual significance of this scene as an artistic representation? There can be no argument about the fact that the *figure in the fresco* is vaulting the bull and there are many other Minoan artistic representations of this same act. The question is not "can it be done?" but "what does it mean?"

I believe we are equipped to answer that question with reasonable accuracy. In consistency with the symbolic context we have explored, the red, vaulting youth should represent the sun-king in the ninth year of his term. He unites with the moon in going through the crescent-shaped horns of the bull. This corresponds with the uniting of sun and moon in the eight year solar-lunar cycle of the calendar. In one sense, the passage of the sun through the horns of the moon is a sacred marriage of the sun-king and the moon-goddess. This sacred union is represented in a parallel fashion by a bronze sun-disc between the horns of a crescent moon in a cult object found in Tylissos near Knossos. (Fig. 33) The date of this bronze emblem is estimated c. 1700-1450 B.C. which is not remote in time from the estimated date of the fresco. (H.M. Gallery VII, Case 97) The similarity between this bronze emblem and the passage of the bronze-colored sun-king through the lunar horns is apparent.[6] We have also seen in Chapter II (Fig. 15) a seal on which an eight-rayed sun-disc appears between the horns of a Minotaur as the *labrys* or double axe does on other seals. The passage of the sun-king through the lunar horns is the significant act that takes place in the Labyrinth.

However, as is usual in Minoan art, the gesture of going through the horns has multiple meanings. We have seen in the discussion of figures 11, 13, 16, and 17 in Chapter II that the *labrys* or double axe is placed between the horns of the bull and that the horns themselves are equated with the pillars of the Labyrinth. To go between these gates of horn is also to go beyond the Pillars of Hercules or, in other words, to go to one's death in the Labyrinth. Therefore, going between the bull's horns means a sacred union with the goddess, not here on earth, but in the hereafter. And that is why a maiden appears between the horns in the picture. She wears the black boots or buskins of a sacred king, relating to his vulnerable heel—and later adopted in Greek tragedy by the tragic hero. She stands between the horns to signify the death aspect of the Great Goddess.

The wearing of boots or buskins by sacred kings and later

by the protagonist in Greek drama is a curious business. Robert Graves has explored the subject in depth in *The White Goddess*. A complete exposition of how the custom developed and its many ramifications would take us too far afield. But essentially the idea is that a sacred king was identifiable by a vulnerable heel—such as Achilles had—or a lame club-foot—such as OEdipus had—that obliged him to walk on the toes with one foot, keeping the sacred heel from touching the ground. Accordingly such a foot is much like the foot of a bull, the fetlock or heel being raised from the ground and unused. Graves believes that this effect was produced by deliberately laming sacred kings.[7] We have previously seen that the smith-god, Hephaistos, had a lame leg and that Talos, the twin of Herakles, was a sun-king of an equivalent type. The bull-foot also had phallic significance and its insertion into a boot became a symbol of a sacred sexual union. Talos was not lame, but there is good evidence that sacred Minoan kings who represented him wore boots or buskins to simulate the phallic foot.

The boots of the sacred king are a frequent motif in Minoan art. An excellent example of the motif may be seen on a gold ring from a tholos tomb at Arkhanes in Crete. (Fig. 34) The ring is dated c. 1400-1350 B.C. which means that it is approximately contemporary with the Toreador Fresco (H.M. Gallery VI, case no. 88). It features six figure-of-eight shields and two pairs of boots disposed antithetically on either side of a knobbed sceptre. There can be no reasonable doubt that the boots are included on this ring as badges of the sacred king since they are displayed with figure-of-eight shields, long known to be a symbol of the king, and a sceptre or staff of office. The sceptre is probably knobbed to signify the buds on a living bough of a sacred tree.

Convincing additional evidence is provided by the Chieftan's Cup from Agia Triada. (Fig. 35) This well-preserved cup is dated c. 1700-1450 B.C., a little earlier than the ring discussed above but close enough to be significant. (H.M. Gallery VII, case no. 95) The cup shows a young sacred king standing before a shrine, sceptre in hand. He wears the belt and loin cloth of a bull-vaulter just as the sacred king does in the relief fresco discussed in Chapter V. (Fig. 24) He also resembles the king in the fresco in that he wears a necklace, doubtless a royal emblem, and has long tresses like a bull-vaulter. Opposite him is a man in a helmet with a sword at his shoulder and a large "sprinkler," a ritual object, in his other hand. On the opposite side of the cup, which is not visible in Figure 34, are three men bringing the hides of sacrificed bulls to the sacred king. Below the figures, the base of the cup is striped with eight bands to symbolize the eight year cycle of the solar-lunar calendar. And finally, the pertinent detail to note is that the sacred king wears high boots with five bands on the upper parts in honor of the five-fold Goddess.

The vaulting position of the sun-king is also meaningful. His back is arched so that he nearly describes a circle, his feet descending to join his hands. This motif—a very frequent one in Minoan art—should be familiar. One version is the bull-lion circle previously discussed and illustrated.

But let us look at one more example of this motif which is especially pertinent in the present context. It may be seen on an engraved gem of the Late Minoan Age which is in the Ashmolean Museum. (A.M. 1938. 1071) (Fig. 36) The stone comes from the sacred Psychro Cave in Crete and therefore from a religious context. In describing it, V. E. G. Kenna associates the arched figure of the engraving with the Minoan bull-vaulting sport.[8] It shows a Minotaur with a bull's head and forelegs and a man's torso and legs. The figure is arched backward so that the legs and the forelegs nearly meet, exactly paralleling the position of the vaulting figure in the fresco. In the field there is also a figure-of-eight shield, a symbol of the sacred king, and an impaled triangle, which probably symbolizes the union of the male and female principles.

What is the significance of the sacred sun-king in this position? He has passed between the horns and into death where he is joined with the female principle as the impaled triangle suggests. But as we have amply seen before, the circular position signifies eternal return and, hence, an end which is also a beginning. Ariadne promises her sacred kings rebirth after death and this symbol represents the transitional stage before rebirth.

The maiden at the right of the picture stands ready with open arms to receive the vaulter after he completes his circle on Ariadne's island—as it were—and returns to this world to be reborn. That a maiden is to be found in this position on the fresco is again significant since she represents the Great Goddess in her aspect as life-giver. The entire cycle is now complete. The picture as a whole is emblematic of the sacred marriage of the sun-king and the moon-goddess, of his death, and of his union with her after death, and finally of his rebirth through her.

What remains to be done is to relate this symbolic ritual to the calendar festival in which in some fashion it must have been performed or mimetically simulated. All the evidence points to the mid-summer festival during the ninth year of the king's reign following an eight year cycle of the calendar. I refer to the fourteen Halcyon Days discussed in Chapter V.[9] At that time, in the seventh lunation following a great year, the summer solstice is followed eleven days later by a full moon which occurs precisely on the last day of the fourteen day festival.[10] The full moon, as we have seen, is the Great Goddesses' central phase and is represented by Hera, the goddess as mother. It is certainly appropriate that the Herakles-bull should die at summer solstice when the sun begins to wane and at full moon, Hera's symbol, the mother of Herakles.

Additional evidence that the bull-vaulting ritual took place during the summer festival is provided by the seal discussed in Chapter II on which the sport is depicted. This seal (Fig. 19) shows a bull with head and forelegs mounted on the corner of a labyrinth design. The vaulter is shown in the beginning of his somersault over the bull's back. In the light of what we know about the position of festivals in the labyrinth of the calendar, the placement of bull and vaulter at this particular corner of the labyrinth design is surely significant. Bull and vaulter are mounted upon the upper right hand corner of the labyrinth which is precisely where the summer festival of seven days is indicated on the calendar. The seal plainly tells us that this is the festival of the year when bull-vaulting takes place.

If Minoan or Creto-Mycenaean kings of Knossos were literally sacrificed in a fertility ritual, the event would logically occur at this festival. And if an Athenian prince named Theseus actually slew a sacred king or a sacred bull representing him and married a princess of Knossos, the event and the related ceremony would have occurred at this time. We may recall that the seven youths and seven maidens whom the myth tells us Theseus led to Knossos make fourteen in all, corresponding with the fourteen Halcyon Days and that they were demanded by Minos every eight years or in the ninth year of his reign. The fourteen Athenians may have been intended as yearly sacrifices, a youth and a maid each year, as surrogates for the king in the seven year period following their arrival, the eighth year being the end of the king's great year term and the time of his own sacrificial death. But, of course, this can not be proved or disproved.

It appears more likely that in the Late Bronze Age with which we deal, the primitive blood sacrifice of tribute victims and kings had been superseded by a mimetic ritual game of bull-vaulting which simulated the death of the king and that afterwards the bull was sacrificed in the name of the king. Whether the participating celebrants entered a ring with a live bull or whether they somersaulted over a substitute of some sort—perhaps a man in a bull's head-and-hide costume—can not be determined and it is futile to speculate upon the question. But the symbolic import of the ritual is essentially clear whatever its means of attainment may have been.

It is likely that a related ritual, perhaps less elaborate, was celebrated at the midsummer seven day festival every year when the Herakles-bull season ended and the Talos-lion season began. It would be Talos, the bronze man, who might be expected to ritually slay the Herakles-bull. It is therefore probable that the red-bronze, vaulting figure in the calendar fresco is none other than Talos himself. And it is not unlikely that the dance which

Lucian called "Talos the bronze-sentinel of Crete" is being performed before our eyes in the center of the calendar fresco. If this identification is correct, he is doubtless called a "sentinel" because he guards a boundary of the solar year just as the two-headed Roman god, Janus, did. The boundary, of course, is the summer solstice when the reign of his twin, Herakles, must end.

The bull-vaulting dance of Talos is essentially a tragic dance since it is a *mimesis* of love, death, and rebirth. For the true tragic rhythm does not end on the down beat of death but on the rising beat of transcendence and regeneration. It does, indeed, mean a temporal death, for the bull must die, but he is reborn as Talos, the vaulter. It is not surprising that Ernest Hemingway saw in Spanish bull-fighting a tragic drama of love and death. The Spanish sport was imported to Rome by the Emperor Claudius who brought it from Thrace and from thence it was introduced into Spain.[11] It is interesting that to this day the matador who kills his bull with outstanding courage and grace is awarded the *pata* or foot of the bull. The foot of the bull, of course, was the emblem of the sacred king in Minoan Crete. It is more than likely that Thracian bull-fighting was originally a ritual dance brought to Thrace from Minoan Crete.

The annual summer festival may have corresponded with the spring festival celebrated on Delos where Theseus and the youths and maidens reputedly danced the Crane Dance after their deliverance from Knossos. But it is more likely that the Delos festival corresponded with the spring festival at Knossos. The Crane Dance, as it has been shown, is clearly distinguishable from the vaulting dance of Talos. Yet it has a similar theme. The initiation ritual of which it was a part marked the end of childhood and the beginning of maturity for the youths and maidens participating. It was thus related to the theme of death and rebirth—the end of one stage of life and the beginning of another. And since it was a courting dance, it was also related to love and marriage. The triple theme of love, death, and rebirth thus complemented the theme of the fourteen day festival which was held at the end of a king's term.

It is indeed surprising how so many seemingly diverse cultural by-products can be traced back to a common origin in the ritual celebration of this triple theme. And it is also surprising to find how many of these survive in some form to this very day. We still celebrate the Olympic Games and the fact that they are held only every four years is a survival of the four year half-cycle of the calendar's great eight year cycle. Classical Greek tragedy is still very much alive and is performed before modern audiences in the impressive ancient outdoor threatre at Epidaurus in the Peloponnese. The nucleus from which it grew can be traced back to the rituals performed in the theatral area at the Palace of Knossos and other similar theatres in Minoan Crete. The Labyrinth dance of Theseus and Ariadne has also survived to the present day in several variant forms performed by country folk. The so-called Troy dance, a spiralling figure, is still a country dance in Mediterranean lands and is quite apparently a derivative from the Labyrinth dance. In a taverna in Nauplion on the Bay of Argos I watched sailors dance an intricate figure involving turnings and returnings and parallel movements of two lines while locked together by arms and wrists which closely resembled the description of the dance which Homer says the youths and maidens danced at "spacious Knossos for Ariadne of the lovely hair." Was it the same dance that was already very ancient in Homer's time? Who could be certain that it was? And who could be certain that it was not? Finally, bull-fighting still maintains its fascination and shows no sign of dying out in Spain and Latin American countries. Nor has it lost its original tragic theme as a game of love and death.

Figure 28
Sketch of seal design. From Zakros. Late Minoan I or II. HM. Gallery IX, Case 124. Lion-Griffon-Bull united by sacral knot.

Figure 29
Fresco fragment from Knossos. Priestess or Goddess wearing sacral knot behind her neck.

Figure 30
Late Minoan Talismanic gem from East Crete. AM. 1938.984.
Two serpents surmounting rustic shrine of two pillars with
pierced egg within.

Figure 31
Late Minoan Talismanic gem from Siteia. AM. 1938.985. Two pillared shrine with baetylic pillar within.

Figure 32
Late Minoan gold signet ring from Knossos. AM. 1938.1127.
Goddess mourning dying god by two-pillared shrine containing
baetylic pillar shaped like a double axe.

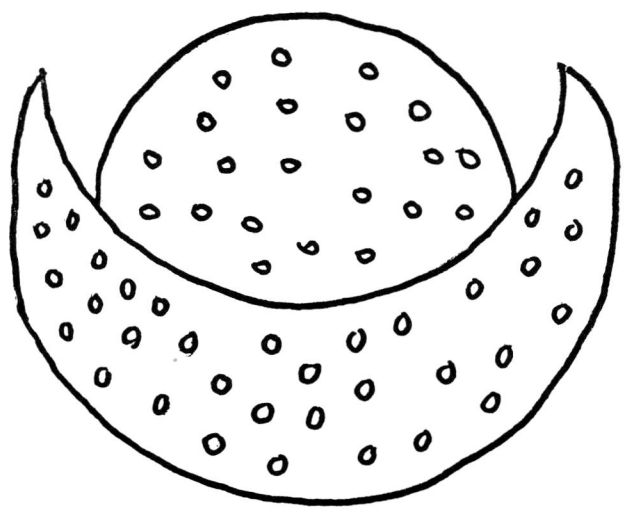

Figure 33
Bronze sun-disc and crescent moon. Cult object from Tylissos (c. 1700-1450 B.C.). HM. Gallery VII, Case 97.

Figure 34
Gold signet ring from tomb at Arkhanes (c. 1400-1350 B.C.).
Sacred boots of Priest-King with figure-of-eight shields and sceptre.

Figure 35
Cup showing ritual scene from Agia Triada (c. 1700-1450 B.C.). A soldier with a sword and ritual sprinkler facing the Priest-King at right who holds staff of office and wears necklace and five-banded sacred boots. Below, the cup shows eight bands to signify an eight year reign.

Figure 36
Late Minoan gem from Psychro Cave. AM. 1938.1071. Man-bull in circle of eternal return with figure-of-eight shield and impaled triangle.

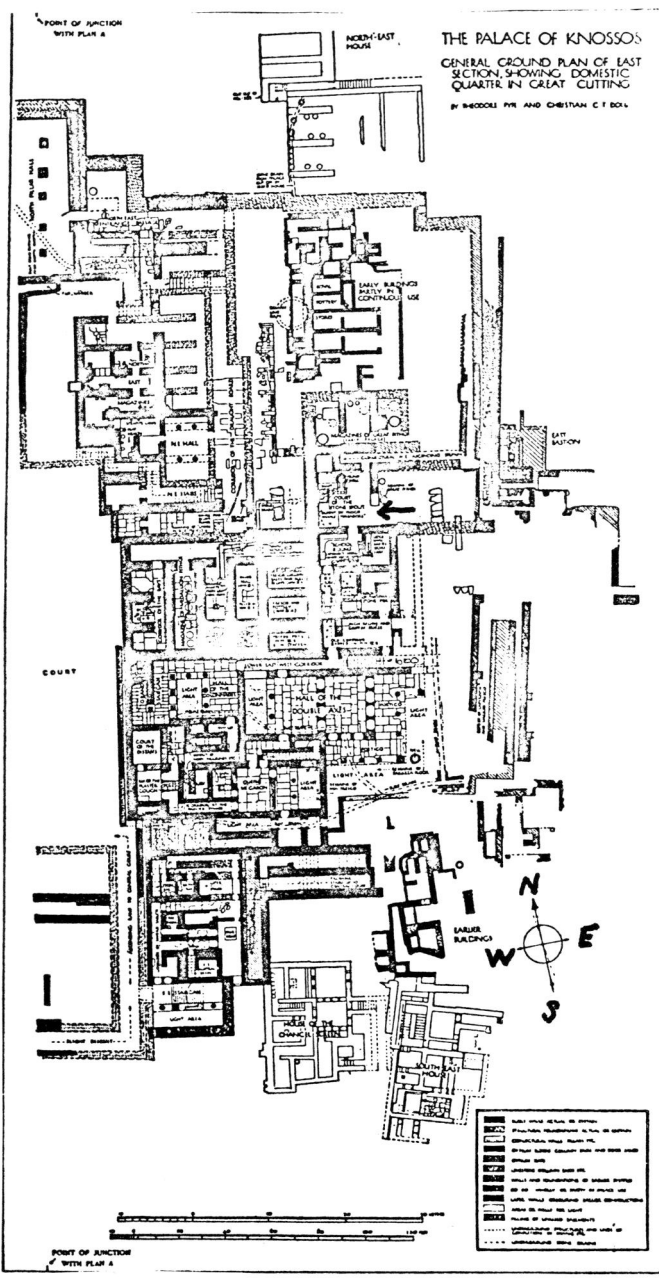

Figure 37
East wing of the Palace of Knossos. Arrow indicates location of the Court of the Stone Spout where Toreador Fresco was found.

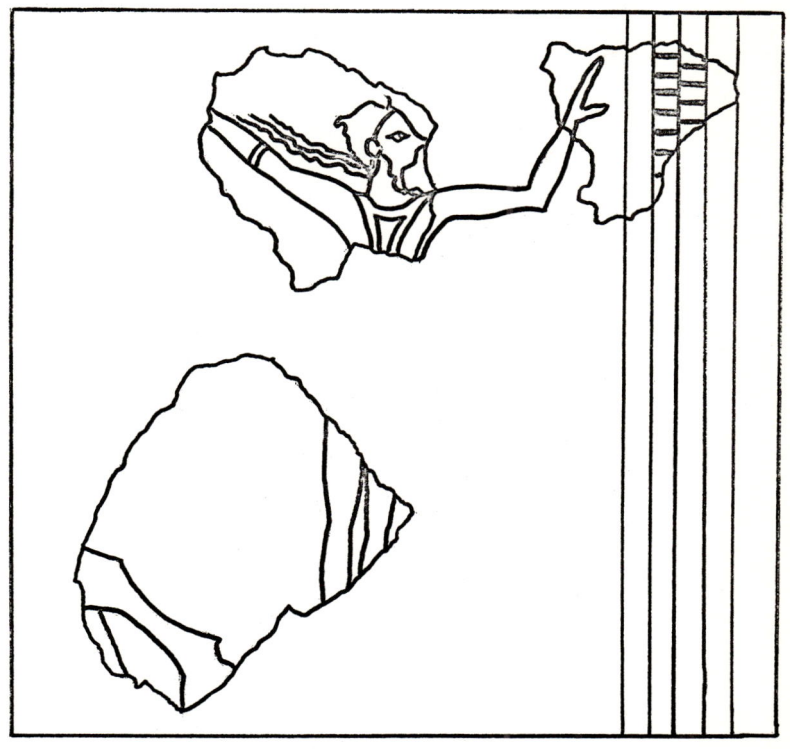

Figure 38
Fragment of fresco from Court of the Stone Spout of the Palace of Knossos. Male bull-vaulter alighting. Bull's hind legs visible at left.

Figure 39
Fragment of fresco from Court of the Stone Spout of the Palace of Knossos. Female toreador between bull's horns.

Figure 40
Fragment of fresco from Court of the Stone Spout of the Palace of Knossos. Female toreador alighting. Lower border shows moon symbol and four tracks.

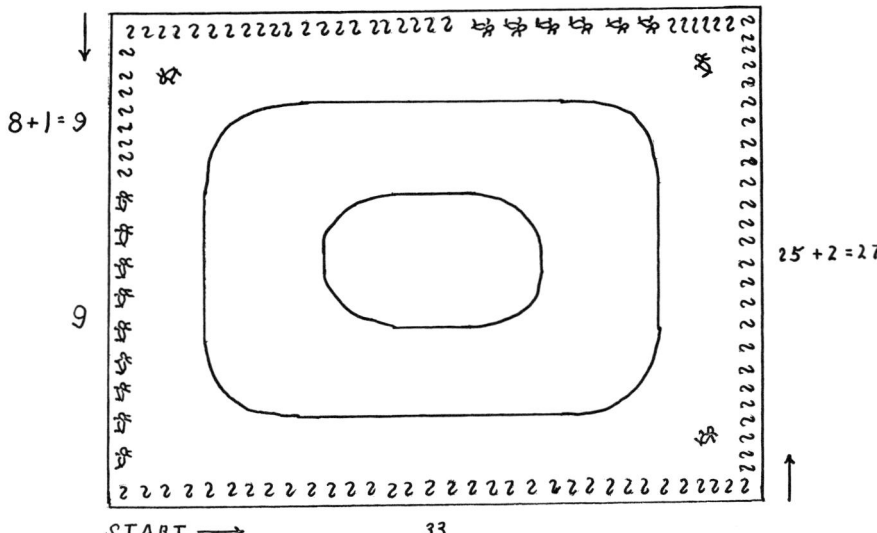

Figure 41
Diagram of clay Table of Offerings from Phaistos. (c. 2000-1700 B.C.) HM. Gallery III, Case 42.

Key
1. 33 lunations = 1/3 of 8 year solar-lunar cycle.
2. 25+2 = 27+33 = 60 lunations = 5 lunar years.
3. 6+60 = 66 lunations = 2/3 of 8 year solar-lunar cycle.
4. 6+66 = 72 lunations = 6 lunar years.
5. 21+72 = 93 lunations = 26 June of 8th year of solar-lunar cycle which is last day of spring season followed by summer festival on Toreador Fresco calendar.
6. 9+93 = 102 lunations = spring equinox (March 20) of 9th year of calendar.
7. 9+102 = 111 lunations + 1/2 lunation to full moon = 111 1/2 lunations = 1/2 saros (18 years + 11 1/3 days is one full saros) 223 lunations = 1 saros (period governing solar and lunar eclipses).

TABLE OF MEASUREMENTS

A	B	C	D	E	F	G	H
Track	Border length in inches	*Av. marks per inch	Inches of border missing	Number of existing marks	Total marks estimated	Estimated marks + existing marks	Marks on Plate IV
L.V.-1	7.75"	6.5	4	25	4X6.5=26	51	51
L.V.-2	7.75"	6.3	4	24	4X6.3=25.2	49.2	49
L.V.-3	7.75"	6.3	3.6	26	3.6X6.3=22.68	48.68	49
L.V.-4	7.75"	6.5	3	31	3X6.5=19.5	50.5	51
R.V.-1	7.75"	6.5	4.5	23	4.5X6.5=29.25	52.25	52
R.V.-2	7.75"	6.3	2	37	2X6.3=12.6	49.6	49
R.V.-3	.7.75"	6.3	1.75	38	1.75X6.3=11.025	49.025	49
R.V.-4	7.75"	6.5	2.875	33	2.875X6.5=18.6875	51.6875	51
T.-1	25.25"	6	12.5	75	12.5X6=75	150	150
T.-2	25.25"	6.3	11	91	11X6.3=69.3	160.3	160
T.-3	25.25"	6	8	102	8X6=48	150	150
T.-4	25.25"	6.3	9.1	103	9.1X6.3=57.33	160.33	160
B.-1	25.25"	5.5	24.3	6	24.3X5.5=133.65	139.65	140
B.-2	25.25"	5.2	23	10	23X5.2=119.6	129.6	130
B.-3	25.25"	5.2	21.75	17	21.75X5.2=113.1	130.1	130
B.-4	25.25"	5.5	23.25	12	23.25X5.5=127.875	139.875	140

* Based on measurable samples. Some existing marks are on fragments too small to permit practical measurement.

Figure 42

Figure 43
The Court of the Stone Spout where the Toreador Fresco was found.

NOTES

[1] Graves, *White Goddess*, p. 132.
[2] There is good evidence in Plutarch that the games at Olympia were held long before the first recorded celebration in 776 B.C. Fordsdyke, *Greece Before Homer*, p. 39.
[3] Forsdyke, *Greece Before Homer*, p. 127.
[4] See discussion in Chapter VI.
[5] Willetts, *Cretan Cults and Festivals*, pp. 112-113.
[6] The example illustrated is not unique. A similar object in stone is described in the Heraclion Museum catalogue as "a sacred symbol which combines the solar disc and a crescent moon." Alexiou, *Guide to the Archaeological Museum of Heraclion*, p. 54. Gallery IV, Case 52, No. 491.
[7] Graves, *White Goddess*, p. 355.
[8] Kenna, *Cretan Seals*, p. 135.
[9] See discussion in Chapter V.
[10] It is interesting that the Parian Chronicle (c. 300 B.C.) dates the Fall of Troy in the ninth year of the siege on the seventh day from the end of Thargelion. And according to several ancient mythographers, it fell at full moon. Those who agreed with the Parian Chronicles, but placed it in the following month, made it fall on July 4. This date is so close to the date indicated by the calendar for the end of the reign of a sacred king that it ought to be noted. Notice that Troy was supposed to have fallen during the ninth year of the siege, which corresponds with the ninth year of a king's reign, and that it fell at full moon, as the corresponding calendar festival does, and that it fell seven days after the end of a month, while the festival ends seven days after the end of a season, and that the absolute date in modern terms is given as July 4 by the mythographers, while my interpretation of the calendar places

the end of this festival on July 2. My point, of course, is not that Troy actually fell on this date, but that legend made it fall on this date to coincide with a calendric tradition that sacred kings, such as Priam probably was, should die at this time. Forsdyke, *Greece Before Homer*, p. 55 and p. 61.

[11] Graves, *White Goddess*, p. 357.

Chapter X

DAIDALOS

It is generally believed that the Labyrinth of Knossos is none other than the royal Palace itself. The reasoning is that the Palace is an extremely complex structure with many rooms and passageways resembling a maze or labyrinth and that the Greeks of Theseus' day who ferried the victims of the Minotaur to Crete preserved the memory of this intricate edifice. One could add to the argument that the *labrys* or double axe may be seen as a mason's mark on some of the stones of the building, and that therefore the place of the *labrys* or the Labyrinth is the building itself.

I believe that anyone who has been following the thread of this book has already discovered that this explanation will not do. The deciphering of the Linear B tablet that mentions a specific sanctuary called the "Labyrinthos" is alone enough to dispell this notion not to mention the symbolic significance of the Labyrinth which we have been exploring in depth. But if the Palace itself is not the Labyrinth of Knossos, precisely where was its location? I believe a more convincing explanation than the generally accepted one may be found by examining the spot where the Toreador Fresco was discovered.

In the spring of 1970 I had the opportunity to explore the excavations at Knossos for several days with this specific problem in mind. The fragments of the Toreador Fresco were found together with fragments of three other frescoes in the so-called "Court of the Stone Spout" and on the west side of the adjoining room which was originally labelled the "School Room" but which has been renamed the "Potter's Worshop."[1] The Court of the Stone Spout was so named because of a stone spout projecting from its west wall 73 inches above the flagstone floor level and emptying into a blind drain. The adjoining room was originally called a school room by Evans because of the benches running along its wall, but it has now been labelled the Potter's Worshop because of the ceramic vessels which were found in it. (Fig. 37)

This section of the Palace is on the east side of the Great Central Court and is known as the Domestic Quarter. Archaeological evidence shows that this quarter was of late construction being a part of the Last Palace and dated by pottery as after Late Minoan III b.[2] The fresco fragments found here, however, were clearly not on the walls of either the Potter's Workshop or the existing walls of the Court of the Stone Spout. Evans discovered them in 1901 at a level that would be above one's head if one stands on the floor of the excavated court. He describes his find as follows: "They were found near the South-West Corner of this little court [the Court of the Stone Spout] and mostly at a mean height of about a metre and a half above its terrace level. By all appearance they must have been derived from an upper room, perhaps partly superposed on the fine Ante-Chamber that preceded the later lower-floor arrangements to which belonged the so-called 'School Room'."[3]

Evans thought that these frescoes were in a loggia over the "School Room" and of much earlier date than the reconstructed rooms and court below, which are still extant. In other words, he inferred the existence of an upper story, above the Domestic Quarter, and opening out upon the Court of the Stone Spout, which was open to the sky and served as a light well. Of this upper story nothing remains standing today. Evans' inference seems a sound conjecture for two reason. First because the stratigraphy shows that the fresco fragments were found at a level high above the present terrace floor and secondly because works of art of this quality would hardly have decorated the walls of the little workshop rooms of the domestic servants of the Palace housed on the lower floor.

However, his view that this upper level was of earlier date than the construction of rooms below it is questionable. The fragments of the Toreador Fresco were found among bits of pottery dated stylistically as Late Minoan II according to Evans' account.[4] Yet he originally dated the fresco as Late Minoan I a or "shortly preceding 1500 B.C." This estimate he later revised downward to Late Minoan II. But since the structure below the hypothetical story which presumably housed the frescoes was built after Late Minoan III b, it appears that a still later date is more likely to be correct. In short, a date contemporary with the Linear B tablets found in the Palace.

The room or loggia looking out on the open Court of the Stone Spout must have been a place of some special significance to have on its walls not only one but four frescoes. The fragments of the other three frescoes found at the same site are enlightening. Unfortunately, not enough fragments of the other three frescoes were preserved to make possible complete reconstructions. Yet the existing fragments reveal unmistakably the pictorial theme with which they dealt. It was bull-vaulting.

One shows a male vaulter with arms outstretched for balance in the act of alighting behind the bull whose hind legs may be seen and clearly identified. (Fig. 38) Part of the right hand vertical border of this fresco is preserved and it contains a blue and an orange track striped with horizontal bars recalling the border of the calendar. Whether the border had four tracks, as the calendar has, can not be determined from the existing fragment which may or may not represent the complete horizontal width of the border.

The fragments of a second fresco show a female figure grasping a bull's horns. (Fig. 39) She appears to correspond with the female figure on the left side of the calendar fresco who is also placed between the bull's horns. None of the border of this fresco has survived.

The fragments of the third other fresco show a female figure who appears to be in an alighting position corresponding to the right-hand female figure in the calendar fresco. (Fig. 40) No parts of a bull appear in the existing fragments but segments of the upper and lower horizontal borders are preserved. The upper border shows an orange and a blue track marked with bars. The lower border appears to be preserved in its entire width. It has four tracks marked with bars—two blue tracks and two orange ones—and in the center runs what appears to be a sequence of moon symbols such as we have in the calendar fresco. The upper border is probably incomplete in width since we might expect it to have four tracks and moon symbols between them just as the lower border has.

This lower border is so nearly similar to the calendar fresco border that it is evident that it represents the same motif. There are some differences but they are not material. The moon symbols point in the opposite direction from those on the bottom of the calendar fresco and the color sequence of the tracks is like that of the top border of the calendar rather than like the corresponding lower border. Only one blue moon symbol is preserved and the forward tip of a white symbol which precedes it. The white symbol succeeds the blue symbol on the calendar fresco as well. The fact that the sequence here reads in the opposite direction from the calendar is not material since, as we have seen, the symbols may be read in reverse. The most remarkable similarity, however, is that the number of bars on the lower two tracks which are preserved for the length of the blue moon symbol from the convex tip of the white symbol to the convex tip of the blue one is six, which corresponds with the average number of day marks on the calendar for one moon phase.

Before coming to any conclusion about the significance of these similarites in motif, we should look farther afield. No other fresco found at Knossos has a border that corresponds so closely to the calendar fresco border as the fragment illustrated in Figure 40. But two other fragmentary frescoes found in different locations in the Palace have portions of border designs remaining which in terms of design tradition have something in common with the border of the calendar fresco. One shows a Pillar Shrine with Horns of Consecration and Double Axes stuck into columns. (H.M. no. 21) The fragments of its preserved border show a sequence of rosettes paralleled above and below by pairs of orange and blue tracks marked with bars. Another fragmentary fresco shows a Central Pillar Shrine. A small fragment of its top border is preserved. (H.M. no. 10) It consists of two tracks, one orange and one blue, both marked with bars.

Considered simply as a stylized artistic motif these borders have something in common with the border of the calendar fresco. And if we go even farther afield we may find other examples of the kind. The Agia Triada Sarcophagus (H.M. Gallery XIV, case 171) has a recognizably related border design, the Tiryns Procession Fresco (N.A.M. no. 5883) in Athens does also, and the Tiryns Bull Fresco (N.A.M. no. 1595). These fresco borders display variations on an artistic motif which has been adopted from calendric iconography but which has been applied conventionally for the sake of tradition. This tradition of calendric iconography is also to be found, as we have seen, on many Minoan seals and other objects of art. And as we have also seen, the tradition goes back in Crete to origins in Minoan religion that ante date the Knossos Calendar itself. The Knossos Calendar is a Late Bronze Age work and it may well enough have had predecessors that have not survived.

The conclusion to be drawn is that a distinction must be made between the Toreador Fresco, which is a calendar as well as a symbolic work of art, and frescoes or other works of art which conventionally incorporate motifs that have been derived from icons of a solar-lunar religion. All of the frescoes discussed above, with the possible exception of the one illustrated in Figure 40, appear to me to belong in the latter category.

Let us return now to the frescoes found together at the Court of the Stone Spout. Evans thought that the difference in style evident in these four frescoes indicated a later date for the more crudely executed ones.[5] The two frescoes illustrated in Figures 38 and 39 appear to be by different artists and both are relatively crude in execution by comparison with the one illustrated in Figure 40. Whether the more crudely done frescoes were painted later, as Evans thought, or earlier, as might also be argued, is less important than the fact that the difference in style suggests different artists and probably different dates for these works. Even if they were all painted during the period of the Last

Palace (c. 1400 - 1200 B.C.), as seems likely, there would have been about a two hundred year period in which various artists could have made their contribution to a common theme.

If we assemble the evidence which we have now reviewed, we should be able to draw some conclusions from it. The calendar fresco was found at the same place and on the same stratigraphic level as the fragments of three other frescoes. All four frescoes appear to have been originally on the walls of a single room or loggia above the west wall of the Court of the Stone Spout and near the south corner of that wall. All the frescoes share a common theme, bull-vaulting, and two have borders which repeat motifs found also on the calendar fresco. The four frescoes appear to have been painted at different times by different hands. Finally, all four frescoes appear to belong to the Last Palace to which the Linear B tablets also belong.

One of the Linear B tablets mentions a sanctuary called the "Labyrinthos." We might expect such a sanctuary to be adorned with religious icons appropriate to the theme which we have discovered that the labyrinth as a motif reflects. No other concentration of frescoes found at Knossos fits this need better than the Calendar Fresco and the three other frescoes found with it. The conclusion to be drawn is that the Labyrinthos of Knossos was located on a loggia above the west wall of the Court of the Stone Spout and that the Calendar Fresco was its central feature.

The representation of a common theme by different artists over a period of years in a holy sanctuary is not at all unlikely. There are plenty of examples of the like in Medieval and Renaissance Christian chapels and cathedrals. Indeed, it is rather what we should expect in a sanctuary as important as the Labyrinthos must have been at Knossos. It would be from this sanctuary and its calendar that all of the religious festivals and rituals of the year would be governed. Observation of the calendar and observation of the sun, moon, and stars would certainly have been a function of priests or priestesses of this sanctuary.

I believe this is the explanation of its location. The vast Palace at Knossos is built upon a hill and the eastern wing is terraced on a slope which drops off into a valley and stream bed. The best place to observe the heavens with an unobstructed view, and most especially the sun rising in the east, would be on an upper level of the Palace structure in the terraced east wing from the west side of an open court. This precisely fits the location where we have, on other grounds, inferred that the Labyrinthos must have been. And for this reason, as well as for the need for light in any case, it is most likely that the Labyrinthos was an open Loggia with eastern exposure to the light well of the Court and with a view of the rising sun and the night skies. In fact, it is probable that the Labyrinthos constituted a kind of astronomical observatory as well as a sanctuary.

Who might we expect should perform such astronomical observations? A priest, no doubt, but who by name? There could be no more likely candidate than Daidalos himself. Are we not told that Daidalos designed the Labyrinth and built it. Could he have designed so intricate a maze as the Calendar Fresco represents without carefully observing the solstices of the sun and the phases of the moon? But, of course, I speak figuratively when I say Daidalos himself made these observations. They must have been made over a long period of time by generations of priests of Daidalos taught in a lore that the mythic hero Daidalos was supposed to have fathered. We know from a Linear B tablet that there was a sanctuary at Knossos called the "Daidaleion." The likelihood is that there was a guild of artist-craftsmen-engineers who also had status as priests and astronomers and who may have been called "Daidalidai" much as the trained guild of bards of later date were called "Homeridai" in honor of Homer. A "guild" of craftsmen did exist in Athens in classical times and they were called "Daidalidai" and claimed descent from Daidalos.[6] Since the Athenian tradition almost certainly had its roots in Minoan Knossos, we may confidently infer that a fraternity of Daidalidai or priests of Daidalos were associated with the "Daidaleion" at Knossos.

NOTES

[1] Evans, *Palace of Minos*, Vol. III, p. 210 and p. 233.
[2] Palmer, *A New Guide to The Palace of Knossos*, p. 96.
[3] Evans, *Palace of Minos*, Vol. III, p. 210.
[4] Evans, *Palace of Minos*, Vol. III, p. 210.
[5] Mark Cameron and Sinclair Hood, *Catalogue of Plates, Knossos Fresco Atlas* (London, 1967), p. 39.
[6] Willetts, *Cretan Cults and Festivals*, p. 18.

CHAPTER XI

ECLIPSES AND THE HYPERBOREANS

What particular phenomena of astronomy would the priests of Daidalos have been interested in? Given their solar-lunar religion, it would certainly be phenomena concerning the sun and the moon. Aside from the solar-lunar cycle of the calendar, which it is evident they understood, they must inevitably have been struck by the phenomena of eclipses. The event of an eclipse must have appeared to anyone with their religious orientation as a rather serious affair.

Had they any means of predicting or foreseeing probable lunar or solar eclipses? There are a few indications that they may, indeed, have had some knowledge of this sort.

In the Heraclion Museum (Gallery III, Case 42) there is a curious religious vessel which was found at the Palace of Phaistos *in situ* in the shrine in the west court. It is a clay table of offerings with a central hollow to receive libations. (Fig. 41) It is dated c. 2000 - 1700 B.C. The table is rectangular and its border features spirals and bulls in alternate sequences and three bulls in three of the corners.

An analysis of the number of symbols in these sequences yields interesting results. There are 111 symbols in all. Knowing the Minoan propensity for using numbers with a calendric reference in a religious context, we might expect this number to have some significance. Since it is a table for libations, we might also expect that the border symbols should provide a clue to the periods in which libations would be offered.

Is there any correlation between the number 111 and a known astronomical phenomenon? The answer is yes. A cycle of 18 solar years plus 11 1/3 days is known as a *saros*. It is a period or cycle which governs the recurrence of possible eclipses of the sun and the moon. In lunar time it closely approximates 223 synodic months.[1] That is to say 223 average lunations are approximately equal to 18 solar years plus 11 1/3 days or one *saros*. Half of such a cycle, then, would amount to 111 1/2 lunations. This is only a half lunation more than the total number of symbols on the table of offerings. In other words, the table of offerings appears to be symbolically oriented to a half *saros* of nine solar years plus approximately six days.

Now let us see if we find any correlations between the sequences of symbols and the calendar we are familiar with. If we begin at the lower left corner of the table of offerings and count the symbols on the bottom border we find there are exactly 33. This is an interesting number because, if it represent 33 lunations, as we might expect, it amounts to 1/3 of an eight year solar cycle of the calendar or 1/3 of 99 lunations.

Now if we go up the right hand vertical border we find 25 spirals plus 2 bulls in the corners for a total of 27 symbols. This should signify 27 lunations in addition to the 33 we have already counted. If we combine them, we get a total of 60 lunations which is equivalent to exactly 5 lunar years.

Then moving from right to left on the upper border we find 6 spirals at which point the symbol sequence changes to bulls. If we add 6 lunations to the 60 previously counted, we get 66 lunations which is exactly 2/3 of an eight year solar cycle of the calendar. This appears to be an obvious doubling of the first flight of 33 lunations or 1/3 of an eight year solar cycle.

Next we find a sequence of 6 bulls. Add these 6 lunations to the 66 accumulated and the result is 72 lunations or exactly 6 lunar years.

Then we find a sequence of 21 spirals remaining in the upper border. If we add 21 lunations to 72 we get 93 lunations. And this timing also gives us a significant calendar correlation. For if we begin an eight year cycle at new moon on the winter solstice, as the calendar indicates we should, 93 lunations will bring us to the 26th of June of the eighth and final year of the great year cycle. And as we have seen, the 26th of June in this year is the last day of the spring bull-season. It falls five days after the summer solstice, and it is the last day before the beginning of the seven day summer festival. A new moon occurring on this day, which marks the end of a season and the beginning of a festival, is an event that can happen only once in an eight year cycle. As it has been shown, the moon symbols of the calendar can not be continuously in phase with actual lunations as empirically observed, but they have been placed to come into phase periodically at significant intervals.

Moving down the left hand border we find a bull symbol in the corner and a sequence of eight spirals. This gives us 9 lunations to add to the 93 accumulated. The total becomes 102 lunations. This timing also correlates with a significant date. In terms of lunations accumulated on the calendar figured from the first year, it would bring us to the 19th of March in the ninth year. In other words, it would coincide very nearly with the spring equinox in the important ninth year of a sacred king's reign or three months before the fatal Halcyon Days at the summer solstice when his term must end. This, in fact, is the correlation of new moon, spring equinox, and calendar new moon symbol previously noted in Chapter V. Or rather, it is its equivalent, since lunation 102 in year 9 is lunation 3 in year 1 of a new eight year cycle. Since this calendar correlation occurs only once in every eight years, it is certainly significant to find it also indicated on the Phaistos table of offerings.

Remaining to be counted are 9 bull symbols which together with the 102 symbols already counted gives us a total of 111 symbols in all, representing 111 lunations or approximately a half *saros*. Now since the symbols represent complete lunations from new moon to new moon, it follows that an additional half lunation would fall at full moon. And if we added an additional half lunation to the 111 lunations indicated, we would have 111 1/2 lunations which would be 9 solar years and 6 days or almost exactly a half *saros*. It appears to me that the table symbols are meant to be read in this way. The missing half lunation bringing us to full moon seems implied. The maker of the table would not have wished to mar his design by representing a half spiral or a truncated bull. Established custom would have made this unnecessary. Priests performing sacrifices would have known that an extra half lunation to full moon completed the cycle. Furthermore, the fact that there are exactly 18 bull symbols in all leads to the conclusion that the table was oriented to an 18 year *saros* cycle although only a half cycle is represented.

The results of our analysis may be briefly summarized. The table of offerings appears to indicate symbolically when certain libations to the moon-goddess were ceremonially made. The periods are not at random but show, on the contrary, a meaningful correlation with the 18 year plus 11 1/3 day *saros,* the 8 year cycle of the calendar, with lunar years, with the spring equinox, and with one specific calendar date that marks the end of a season and the beginning of the summer festival.

This last correlation is to be particularly noted, since it is not merely a correlation with astronomical facts that might have been known without reference to the particular calendar system contained in the Toreador Fresco. On the contrary, this ceremonial date would have appeared arbitrary had it not exactly correlated with a seasonal festival boundary about which we could have known nothing had it not been revealed by the particular and rather unusual division of seasons in the Toreador Fresco. The correlation of lunation 102 of the table of offerings with lunation 3 of the calendar is also one which verifies our interpretation of the calendar. Not because a new moon approximates the spring equinox in this lunation, a fact which could have been known in any case, but because the new moon symbol on the calendar correlates with this unique event every eight years.

In Chapter V we discovered 11 particular lunations which apparently called for a religious observation of some sort—perhaps libations or sacrifices. The table of offerings points to additional significant lunations which were apparently also celebrated. If we count beyond an eight year cycle to the end of a half *saros,* and therefore repeat certain lunations, we get a total of 19 significant lunations. The significant lunations are as follows: 2, 3, 7, 33, 34, 36, 37, 44, 56, 60, 66, 72, 74, 93, 99, 101, 102, 106, 111. The appearance of 33, 44, 66, 99, and 111 is interesting in the light of the number mysticism previously discussed. All but

111 in this series of five are multiples of 11 and, of course, 111 is only one more than 110 which is 10 x 11. Eleven, as we have seen, is the number of Talos as well as of the goddess. The total of 19 significant lunations corresponds with the nineteenth year in which a full *saros* ends. For a *saros* is 18 years plus 11 1/3 days. And here, also, is our number 11 once more.

A further observation is that lunation 37 at the end of year 3, if a lunation count is carried forward to the end of year 19, is equivalent to lunation 235. Lunation 37 is recognized as significant by a calendar symbol correlation. Therefore, lunation 235 would inevitably be recognized. Lunation 235 is significant because it marks the end of a longer solar-lunar cycle of 19 years, which is known as the Metonic Cycle. It was so named after the Greek astronomer Meton, who officially introduced it into Greek time reckoning in the fifth century B.C. This cycle like the 8 year cycle reconciles solar and lunar time since 19 solar years very nearly equal 235 lunations or 19 lunar years plus 7 lunations. The 7 lunations beyond 19 lunar years would be equivalent to the 7 months which the Knossos calendar would intercalate in 19 solar years. That is in years 3, 6, 8, 11, 14, 16, and 19.

The interesting fact is that this 19 year cycle permits a closer coordination of solar-lunar time than the 8 year cycle. As previously noted, the 8 year cycle will not give an astronomically perfect coordination of new moon and winter solstice at the end of the cycle, since figured on a basis of average lunations there will be an average discrepancy of about a day and a half. But in the 19 year cycle the average discrepancy would be only a fifth of a day or less than five hours.

It seems unlikely that this 19 year cycle was unrecognized by the watchers of the skies who kept solar-lunar time by the fresco calendar. Recently Gerald S. Hawkins, using computer methods, has demonstrated that the builders of Stonehenge I in pre-Celtic Britain were aware of the 19 year cycle and, indeed, were capable of predicting eclipses with great accuracy by stone alignments based upon this knowledge refined to fit the specific conditions at Stonehenge.

An interesting fact about the 19 year cycle is that it also may function as an eclipse cycle. Furthermore, it is an eclipse cycle that is specifically adaptable to reckoning by fixed calendar dates. Professor Hawkins writes, "the metonic cycle of 19 years and the saros of 18 years are both eclipse cycles. The metonic cycle has not been previously recognized as an eclipse cycle, probably because it runs for only 57 years or so. It is, however, a remarkable cycle because eclipses repeat on the same calendar date. The lunar eclipse of December 19, 1964, for example, follows the lunar eclipse of December 19, 1945."[2]

Apparently the people of Stonehenge used a 56 year period divided by a triple-interval measure of $19 + 19 + 18$ years to make their calculations.[3] Stonehenge III C included the erection of a bluestone horseshoe of 19 stones which appears to have symbolized the 19 year cycle. This means that the people of Stonehenge knew the Metonic Cycle and used it to predict eclipses during the period c. 1850 - 1600 B.C., according to Hawkins' dating.

There is considerable evidence that the people of Stonehenge, particularly those of the Wessex Culture, were in contact with peoples from the Aegean and very likely with Mycenaeans or Minoans or both. A number of images of bronze axe blades and daggers of Mycenaean or Minoan type are incised on several stones of the monument as I have seen with my own eyes. The advanced technique of masonry, unparallelled elsewhere in Britain at this date, suggests contact with a culture like Minoan Crete or Mycenaean Greece where a tradition of building in massive stone developed at a contemporary date.

The classical historian Diodorus quotes Hecateus (sixth century B.C.) concerning the fabled Hyperboreans, who by their description appear to be a people who worshipped the sun and the moon at Stonehenge. Hecateus writes, "Opposite to the coast of Celtic Gaul there is an island in the ocean, not smaller than Sicily, lying to the North—which is inhabited by the Hyperboreans, who are so named because they dwell beyond the North Wind." And Hecateus continues, "In this island, there is a magnificent grove of Apollo, and a remarkable temple, of a round form, adorned with many consecrated gifts. . . . The Hyperboreans use a peculiar dialect, and have a remarkable attachment to the Greeks, especially to the Athenians and the Delians, deducing their friendship from remote periods. It is related that some Greeks formerly visited the Hyperboreans, with whom they left consecrated gifts of great value, and also that in ancient times Abaris, coming from the Hyperboreans into Greece, renewed their family intercourse with the Delians. It is also said that in this island the moon appears very near to the earth, that certain eminences of a terrestrial form are plainly seen in it, that Apollo visits the island once in a course of nineteen years, in which period the stars complete their revolutions, and that for this reason the Greeks distinguish the cycle of nineteen years by the name of 'the great year.' During the season of his appearance the God plays upon the harp and dances every night, from the vernal equinox until the rising of the Pleiades. . . ."[4]

Hecateus dates a whole century earlier than Meton who reputedly introduced the 19 year cycle to classical Greece in the fifth century B.C. Although Hecateus does not thoroughly understand the astronomical significance of the cycle, it appears that the Bronze Age Hyperboreans did, and the round temple to Apollo (the sun) certainly fits Stonehenge which we now know to be oriented precisely for the observation of solar and lunar events in a 19 year cycle. The particular mention of contacts between the Hyperboreans and the Bronze Age Greeks of Delos and Athens is also of interest in the light of what we know about Athenian contacts with Knossos contemporary with the Knossos calendar and the tradition that Theseus danced the Crane Dance at Delos in celebration of a solar-lunar religious ritual. Delos, by the way, was the center of a solar cult even in classical times and was with Boeotia one of the few classical Greek areas where the calendar year began with the winter solstice as it does on the Knossos calendar.[5]

We have also seen that there was a cult of the Winds particularly related to Boreas, the North Wind, at Athens in the period of the pre-Greek Pelasgian dynasty and that it was maintained there down to classical times. And on a Linear B tablet from Knossos at the time of the Greek control of the Palace there is testimony of a cult of the Winds with a ministering Priestess. The quotation from Hecateus tells us that the Hyperboreans are so called because they live beyond the North Wind and in a portion not previously quoted he continues, "The supreme authority in that city and the sacred precinct is vested in those who are called Boreadoi, being the descendants of Boreas, and their governments have been uninterruptedly transmitted in this line."[6]

Hecateus mentions a visit made by Greeks to the Hyperboreans and specifically mentions their friendship with the people of Athens and Delos as well as a later visit made by a Hyperborean, Abaris, to renew relations with the Delians.

Contact between the Mycenaean Greeks and the Hyperboreans of the distant-trading Wessex Culture at Stonehenge does not really seem unlikely. And in the light of what we know of both the Knossos calendar and the solar-lunar cult and observatory at Stonehenge, an exchange of astronomical knowledge by peoples who recognized the same divinities does not seem unlikely either. If the dating of Stonehenge is accurate (c. 1900 - c. 1600 B.C. according to Hawkins), the Hyperboreans knew the 19 year cycle as well as how to predict eclipses long before the Mycenaean Greek occupation of Knossos and apparently before the earliest Greek tribes invaded the Balkan Peninsula. The Hyperboreans themselves may have been an Aegean people who migrated westward in stages by way of North Africa and Spain as their own legendary tradition claims. A Mycenaean Greek expedition to the Wiltshire Downs of Britain might have occurred about the time of Stonehenge III. (c. 1600 B.C.) By this date, the Mycenaean Greeks could have adopted a calendar system imported from Minoan Crete which would have had much in common with the system long used at Stonehenge. The Minoan system represented in the Toreador Fresco did not develop suddenly in the period of the last Palace.

The table of offerings from Phaistos, which correlates rather neatly with the fresco calendar, is at least 200 years older than the particular version of the calendar system represented in the fresco. And we have also seen a number of motifs on seals and other objects of art which relate to the fresco motifs or significant calendar numbers but antedate the fresco by 200 years or more. These evidences lead to the inference that the Toreador Fresco calendar had predecessors and is, in fact, a late version of a calendric system long in use in Crete when it was made.

Let us return now to the problem of foreseeing eclipses. If the Minoans knew the length of a *saros*, as it appears they did, could they predict eclipses of the sun and the moon. There is no evidence that they had an elaborate stone constructed solar-lunar observatory of the sort that Stonehenge represents. But they may have known of the 19 year eclipse cycle as well as of the *saros* cycle by c. 1600 B.C. through contact with the Hyperboreans. With this knowledge, supplemented by empirical observations, they could have adapted the 19 year cycle to specific conditions at Knossos. The 19 year cycle, if periodically adjusted, would provide a means of foreseeing theoretically possible eclipses on the basis of calendar dates.

On the other hand, a knowledge of the *saros* alone and a properly kept record of eclipses observed in a sequence of such cycles should have provided them, with the help of a calendar, with a means of predicting with approximate accuracy when the theoretical possibility, but not the certainty, of an eclipse was in the offing. Foreseeing the possibility of a lunar eclipse would have been less difficult for them than predicting eclipses of the sun. They may have observed, as the Babylonians did, that lunar eclipses only occur when the moon is full and when it cuts the apparent path of the sun or the ecliptic.[7] This knowledge combined with their knowledge of the *saros* could have permitted them to foresee possible lunar eclipses with reasonable accuracy. With a knowledge of the *saros*, but lacking modern instruments and additional technical information, they could not have consistently predicted eclipses of the sun. But they could have known, at least, when an eclipse of the sun was theoretically possible. And here again their timing of the event would be approximate rather than perfect.

The table of offerings from Phaistos indicates that the Minoans were aware of the *saros*. Excavations reveal that Knossos was connected with Phaistos by a road which was evidently a main trade route between the two cities and also a route to the Libyan Sea and a port from which ships could sail conveniently to trade with Egypt. The two cities were in close contact culturally and economically at least as early as 1700 B.C., and in the period of the calendar fresco, Phaistos appears to have been under the dominion of the dynasty at Knossos. Therefore, it is likely that if the *saros* was known at Phaistos it was known at Knossos as well, and long known at the time when the calendar fresco was made.

With these connections in view, the question that naturally arises is whether the fresco calendar includes any structural provision for indicating the length of a *saros*. Let us examine the calendar with this question in mind. A *saros* is 18 years plus 11 1/3 days. If we begin to reckon this period from the beginning of an 8 year cycle, we naturally find that the end of the first *saros* will fall 11 1/3 days beyond the starting point of the nineteenth year and that each succeeding *saros* will advance this point up a vertical track by 11 1/3 additional days. The interesting fact is that at the end of 72 years we will have completed nine 8 year cycles or great years at the same time that we are approaching the end of the fourth *saros*.

The end of the fourth *saros* will now fall 45 1/3 days after the end of the seventy-second year, for four times the 11 1/3 day advance equals 45 1/3 days. Now since we are at the beginning of a new 8 year cycle, we will commence the new year on the left hand border omitting the first five days and counting upward from the bottom of the outside orange track. But since we are also interested in where the *saros* will end, we will count up 45 1/3 days to discover where it falls. Since the track has 51 days in all and we have omitted the first five as usual, we will discover that the end of the *saros* falls as nearly as it may be determined in whole days on the last day of the vertical track. For 51 minus 5 equals 46, and since we can not count fractions of days on the calendar, we must count 45 1/3 as 46 days.

Unless this is a coincidence, it appears, then, that the calendar is indicating by the day marks in this track that we have come to the end of the fourth complete *saros*. This, however, is the point at which we ought to expect the calendar to attempt to reconcile 8 year cycles with the 9 year-plus cycles of the half *saros* since 9 and 8 are both factors of 72.[8] It therefore seems unlikely that this correlation is merely a coincidence. It is, of course, not perfect, being 2/3 of a day longer than four complete *saros*. But it is a rather close approximation of the true length of four *saros* and the discrepancy would lessen to something negligible if divided by four in figuring the length of a single *saros*. On the basis of this evidence together with the evidence provided by the Phaistos table of offerings, I am inclined to believe that the Daidalidai of Knossos were aware of the *saros* and could probably predict eclipses within the limitations previously discussed.

We have now travelled a long way through many unexpected turns and twists following the gossamere thread of Ariadne. It has led us through the labyrinth, to the dance of the sun and the moon, to the fabled Minotaur, to Theseus, son of Poseidon, to the very Pillars of Hercules and beyond them to Ariadne's secret island, and even beyond the North Wind to the land of the Hyperboreans. We have explored a realm of mythopoeic thought. And surprisingly we have found there the generative principle—the Swan's egg of Leda—from which the creative energies of Western Civilization were born.

For it is literally, as well as poetically true, that such diverse pursuits as science and poetry, mathematics and music, dancing and drama, religion and athletics—to name but a few—emerged from a common source in mythopoeic thought. Not exclusively from Crete, of course, but from numerous nuclear centers in prehistoric times where mankind thought similarly. Is mythopoeic thought lost to man, superseded by the mechanistic logic of the computer? I think not—or not for long. The substance of thought is forever in flux, but the forms remain the same, and this is as true of forms of synthetic thought—of which myth is but one variety—as it is of analytic thought—of which classical logic is but one variety.

The work of Daidalos, who must have been both scientist and

poet, is not done. And though it is necessary and desirable that we think and act as specialists in our sophisticated age, it is also desirable—and I think even necessary psychically—that we think and act synthetically as human beings. It is a great achievement —and poetically as well as scientifically appropriate—that we may visit the moon-goddess today on the satellite where she mythically resides. But the myth of Daidalos should warn us not to fly too near the sun—as the naive Icarus, son of Daidalos, did—lest it melt our wings of wax—or plastic—and we fall into the abyss.

NOTES

[1] George Sarton, *History of Science* (Cambridge, 1959), p. 120.
[2] Gerald S. Hawkins, *Stonehenge Decoded* (New York, 1965), p. 178.
[3] Hawkins, *Stonehenge Decoded,* p. 140.
[4] Graves, *White Goddess,* p. 309; quotation from Diodorus of Hecateus.
[5] Willetts, *Cretan Cults and Festivals,* p. 108.
[6] Graves, *White Goddess,* p. 309; quotation from Diodorus of Hecateus.
[7] Taton, *History of Science, Ancient and Medieval Science,* p. 117.
[8] The 72 years may have had another significance as well. At the spring equinox the heavens in relation to a viewpoint on earth move in position by about 50 seconds, which in the course of 72 years amounts to 1 degree (50" X 72 = 3600" = 60' = 1°), and in 2160 years amounts to 30 degrees, which is one sign of the Zodiac. This means that in 25,920 years it would be 360 degrees or one complete cycle of the Zodiac. This is known as the "precession of the equinoxes" and it is generally supposed to have been first reported by Hipparchus of Bithynia in the second century B.C. However, there is evidence, which has never been disproved, that the Babylonians, who invented the Zodiac concept, knew how to calculate this phenomenon by the second millennium. B.C. It is possible that the Minoans, who appear to have had knowledge of the spring sign of Taurus, the bull, also knew of the precession of the equinoxes and took it into account every 72 years. Joseph Campbell, *Oriental Mythology* (New York, 1962), pp. 117-118.

APPENDIX

A. The Heraclion Museum Restoration

The existing fragments of the Toreador Fresco may be seen in a restoration in Gallery XIV of the Heraclion Museum. I do not consider this restoration accurate in certain details where it differs from the restoration made under the immediate supervision of Evans and published in the Knossos Fresco Atlas as Plate IX, Second Version.

The Heraclion restoration omits a blue symbol following the black symbol in the lower left-hand corner of the vertical border. Instead, despite the evidence from existing fragments that the blue symbol always follows the black symbol, this restoration places a white symbol at this point. The white symbol is entirely the work of the restorer since there are no fragments existing for any part of it. Furthermore, having omitted the blue symbol, the succeeding sequence of symbols in the left-hand vertical border comes out one less than what we find on the right-hand vertical border. Seven instead of eight. The restorer could not make this error in the right-hand border because the fragments clearly show that the blue symbol follows the black and fragments of all eight symbols exist so that it is impossible to assume that there were only seven. There are, of course, eight symbols in both vertical borders in the Second Version made for Evans. The Heraclion version is obviously inaccurate here.

Another difference is the placement of two small fragments in the right-hand corner of the top border where Evans' Second Version shows none. The placement of these two fragments is arbitrary since there is no join providing evidence that they are correctly placed here. The one at the extreme right shows a small portion of a red symbol above the horizontal border tracks. Apparently on the assumption that this fragment was properly placed, the restorer has filled in a truncated red symbol here and in the corresponding place in the bottom border. Evans' Second Version shows no red symbol here in either the top or bottom border. On the contrary, his pencilled directions on the proof of the First Version in the Ashmolean Museum indicate that the orange symbol alone should fill this space. He has, in fact, briefly sketched the outline of this symbol on the proof of the First Version at the lower right corner because the First Version had omitted all but a small portion of it.

The fact is that there is no evidence either in the form of a join or an analogy with other parts of the border that supports the placement of this small fragment in the upper border at this spot. Since there is no visible join with another fragment, it might very well have been a part of the lower border at either of two positions where a missing red symbol facing the same way with identical tracks below is called for by the sequence but is lacking just such a fragment. In the location where it has been arbitrarily placed it increases the number of symbols in the upper border by less than a whole symbol and, by analogy, calls for another like it in the bottom border despite the lack of fragments to warrant it. For these reasons, I do not consider the Heraclion restored portions of the fresco to be as accurate as Evan's restoration in the Second Version.

However, the preserved fragments in Heraclion must determine any restoration. With the single exception of the two small fragments discussed above, Evans' Second Version agrees with the Heraclion restoration in the placement of all fragments and their joins. The preserved fragments establish two important facts: the upper and lower borders extend beyond the outer edges of the vertical borders, and the color sequence of the tracks in the upper border differs from that in the other borders, being orange, blue, orange, blue rather than orange, blue, blue, orange. Here, also, Evans' Second Version agrees with the facts.

B.   Evans' Proof Correction Notes on the Print of the First Version of the Toreador Fresco Restoration.

Two versions of a restoration of the Toreador Fresco have been published in the Knossos Fresco Atlas. The first version is labelled Plate IX and the second, Plate IX, Second Version. The scale is about one half of the original. The first version was published originally in Evans' *The Palace of Minos*. This version is inaccurate in certain details. Evans noted the inaccuracies on a proof copy of it which provided the basis for the Second Version. This corrected proof is in the Archives of the Ashmolean Museum and I have examined it carefully. There are a number of significant changes that Evans wanted incorporated in the Second Version.

He calls attention to a joint in the fragments of the upper left-hand corner of the border which proves that the top border extends beyond the pillar of the vertical border like a lintel resting on a post. He also points out two fragments showing that a blue wash extended to the left of the vertical border and gave further evidence of the extension of the top and bottom borders beyond the outer edge of the vertical border. This overhang had been clipped off in the first version. He notes the evidence of a similar but longer overhang beyond the outer edge of the right vertical border. His notes call for extensions of the top and bottom borders at the left and at the right to incorporate the fragments clipped from the first version, which had eliminated this overhang. In the lower right-hand corner of the bottom border, he sketched in the portion of the last symbol that had been omitted in the first version.

He noted that there was no junction in the vertical borders which might absolutely establish the vertical height of these borders, but he did not call for any change, probably because it is evident from the proportions of the framed picture, as well as joins with the border, that any possible expansion or contraction vertically would have to be minute. He pointed out the junctions in the upper horizontal border which establish the length of the fresco with precision.

Other changes which he called for showed a concern for the accuracy of the color in restored portions. One such was in reference to the ochre color of the bull which he noted was "too brown" on the first version. He noted that it should be "strong ochre same as border" and drew an arrow pointing to what I have called the "orange" track. This is interesting in the light of the color symbolism of the border and the equation of sun, bull, and orange track.

One other note deserves mention. In reference to the marks which I have identified as day indicators, he notes "scored lines apparently done free hand." It does appear that these lines were painted free hand without a rule to determine their intervals in a mechanical way. My inference is that the painter worked on a mathematical basis rather than a mechanical one in painting them into the appropriate calendar tracks. The spacing is not uniform throughout because different tracks call for differing intervals. Therefore, a ruler with fixed graduations would be too troublesome for a painter to use. Knowing how many day marks were required in each track, a painter would find it easier to fill them in free hand after determining a mid point and subsequent mid points in smaller and smaller subdivisions of the track. It would be a simple calculation to determine how many marks had to be painted in such subdivisions to give the total wanted for the entire track. Thus, the marks could be painted in with the mathematical precision required by the calendar although the spacing of them would be free hand and, therefore, only approximately rather than perfectly regular. Since the marks were put in free hand, the estimate of the number of marks per inch based on existing fragments of the border tracks can only be approximate. However, the results thus obtained are close enough to be significant. The free hand spacing will still be regular enough to provide a basis for an estimate that is likely to be accurate within a margin of plus or minus one mark per track.

C. Table of Measurements (Fig. 42)

The following table shows how the number of day marks were estimated for those portions of each track where existing fragments did not provide them. The results in Column H provided the basis for the diagram of day tracks (Plate IV). The count of existing marks from the fragments and all measurements were based upon Evans' Second Version (Plate II).

BIBLIOGRAPHY

Alexiou, Stylianou. *Guide to the Archaeological Museum of Heraclion*. Athens, 1968.
Atkinson, R. J. C. *Stonehenge*. London, 1960.
Blegen, Carl W. *Troy and the Trojans*. New York, 1963.
Cameron, Mark, and Sinclair Hood. *Sir Arthur Evan's Fresco Atlas,* London, 1967.
Campbell, Joseph. *The Masks of God: Primitive Mythology*. New York, 1968.
―――. *The Masks of God: Occidental Mythology*. New York, 1969.
―――. *The Masks of God: Oriental Mythology*. New York, 1969.
Chadwick, John. *The Decipherment of Linear B*. Cambridge, 1970.
Christoforakis, J. M. *Crete: A Guide*. Athens, 1961.
Cottrell, Leonard. *The Bull of Minos*. New York, 1962.
Dyer, James. *Discovering Archaeology in England and Wales*. Tring, Herts., 1969.
Evans, Sir Arthur. *The Palace of Minos*. 7 Vols. London, 1930.
―――. "Mycenaean Tree and Pillar Cult," *Journal of Hellenic Studies*. 1901.
Forsdyke, John. *Greece Before Homer*. New York, 1964.
Fox, Aileen. *South West England*. New York, 1964.
Frazer, J. G. *The Golden Bough*. London, 1929.
―――. *Pausanias's Description of Greece,* London, 1930.
Graham, J. W. *The Cretan Palaces*. Princeton, 1962.
Graves, Robert. *The White Goddess*. New York, 1948.
―――. *The Greek Myths*. New York, 1959.
Guthrie, W. K. C. *A History of Greek Philosophy*. vol. I. Cambridge, 1962.

Harden, Donald. *The Phoenicians.* New York, 1963.
Harrison, J. C. *Themis.* Cambridge, 1927.
Hawkins, Gerald S. *Stonehenge Decoded.* Garden City. New York, 1965.
Higham, T. F. and C. M. Bowra. *The Oxford Book of Greek Verse in Translation.* Oxford, 1944.
Homer. *The Iliad.* trans. Sir William Marris. Oxford, 1934.
———. *The Odyssey.* trans, E. V. Rieu. Edinburgh, 1955.
Hutchinson, R. W. *Prehistoric Crete.* London, 1962.
James, E. O. *The Cult of the Mother-Goddess.* New York, 1959.
Kenna, V. E. G. *Cretan Seals.* Oxford, 1960.
MacKendrick, Paul. *The Greek Stones Speak.* New York, 1962.
Marinatos, S. and Max Hirmer. *Crete and Mycenae.* New York, 1960.
McDonald, W. A. *Progress into the Past.* Bloomington, Ind., 1969.
Mylonas, George E. *Ancient Mycenae.* Princeton, 1957.
Newall, R. S. *Stonehenge.* London, 1959.
Newman, James R. *The World of Mathematics.* 4 vols. New York, 1956.
Nilsson, M. P. *The Minoan Mycenaean Religion.* Lund, 1950.
———. *The Mycenaean Origin of Greek Mythology.* New York, 1963.
———. *A History of Greek Religion.* Oxford, 1967.
Palmer, Leonard R. *A New Guide to the Palace of Knossos.* New York, 1969.
Pendlebury, J. D. S. *The Archaeology of Crete.* New York, 1965.
Procopiou, Angelo. *Athens, City of the Gods.* New York, 1964.
Sakelloriou, A. and G. Papathanasopoulos. *Guide to National Archaeological Museum, Prehistoric Collections.* Athens, 1965.
Samuel, Alan E. *The Mycenaeans in History.* Englewood Cliffs, New Jersey, 1966.
Sarton, George, *A History of Science.* Cambridge, Mass., 1959.
Stone, J. F. S. *Wessex Before the Celts.* New York, 1958.
Taton, Rene. *History of Science, Ancient and Medieval Science.* New York, 1957.
Taylour, Lord William. *The Mycenaeans.* New York, 1964.
Van Gennep, A. *The Rites of Passage.* London, 1960.

Vermeule, Emily. *Greece in the Bronze Age.* Chicago, 1967.
Virgil. *AEneid.* trans. Davidson, Phila., 1896.
Wace, Helen. *Mycenae Guide.* Meriden, Conn., 1969.
Willetts, R. F. *Cretan Cults and Festivals,* New York, 1962.
———. *Ancient Crete.* Toronto, 1965.

74-8516

```
BL        Herberger, Charles
793       F.
.C7
H47       The thread of
          Ariadne; the
          labyrinth of the
          calendar of Minos
```

DATE			
FEB 28 '75		MAR 05 1997 DEC 04 2001	
APR 08 '75	MAR 01 1986		
DEC 12 1977			
APR 29 '78	MY1 0'87		
AUG 07 1981	APR 22 1987		
AUG 19 1981	MAR 03 '91		
FEB 18 1983	MAR 15		
FEB 11 '06			

WITHDRAWN

PENSACOLA JUNIOR COLLEGE LIBRARY

© THE BAKER & TAYLOR CO.